Never
Too Late

••••••••••••••••••••

Cedar River Daydreams

Other Books by Judy Baer

Never Too Late

Judy Baer

BETHANY HOUSE PUBLISHERS
MINNEAPOLIS, MINNESOTA 55438

Never Too Late
Judy Baer

All scripture quotations are taken from *The Everyday
Bible, New Century Version,* copyright © 1987, 1988 by
Word Publishing, Dallas, Texas 75039.
Used by permission.

Library of Congress Catalog Card Number 92–75599

ISBN 1–55661–329-6

Published by Bethany House Publishers
A Ministry of Bethany Fellowship, Inc.
6820 Auto Club Road, Minneapolis, Minnesota 55438

Printed in the United States of America

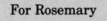

For Rosemary

"If anyone belongs to Christ,
then he is made new.
The old things have gone;
everything is made new!"

2 Corinthians 5:17

Chapter One

"Move over, Leighton." Binky McNaughton jostled Lexi out of the way with her shoulder. "I need to get into my locker."

Lexi shifted to the left and rolled her eyes at the ceiling.

"Move the other way, Lexi," Binky's brother, Egg, pleaded. "You're standing on the math test I dropped."

Lexi lifted her left foot and did her best to ignore her friends. Instead she looked over at Todd Winston, who was shoving books and papers into his locker in an uncharacteristically sloppy manner. He banged the locker door shut with his elbow and ran his fingers through his blond hair.

"Hey, Todd!" Lexi raised her voice over the hallway din. "What's the hurry?"

"I have to work at my brother Mike's garage. He told me to be there *immediately* after school." Todd glanced at his watch. "I'm late. Mr. Raddis kept us after class. Mike is expecting me."

"Haven't you been working at the garage a lot lately? I thought this was supposed to be a part-time job."

"Mike's been taking time off," Todd admitted.

"I thought Mike practically lived at that garage."

"Well, he's finally got a reason to leave." A grin spread across Todd's even features, and his blue eyes began to twinkle. "He's got a girlfriend."

"What's this about a girlfriend?" Egg included himself in the conversation.

"A new girl?" Binky joined the group. "Mike? Is it serious?"

Egg and Binky McNaughton were two of Todd and Lexi's closest friends, a quirky pair who spent a lot of their time in good-natured bickering. Binky and Egg were their own best friends—and worst enemies.

Egg was tall and lean; Binky, tiny. She reminded Lexi of the sparrows that ate in the bird feeder outside the Leightons' kitchen window. Binky was always jumping from one topic or crisis to another, just like a little bird after bits of seed.

Todd interrupted Lexi's thoughts. "Mike has met a great girl."

"Tell us about her," Binky demanded. "This is *so* romantic. I love romantic things. Don't you?"

"How do you know it's romantic?" Egg shot back. "You've never even seen this person. You don't know how much Mike likes her. Maybe it's not romantic at all."

Binky glared at her brother. "Mike's not at the shop. He's having his brother work for him, which means he's probably seriously in love. *That's* romantic."

Egg rolled his eyes and Todd laughed. "Actually, Egg, I think Binky's right this time. My brother's been acting pretty lovesick."

"What's she like?" Binky asked, even more enthusiastic now that Todd had confirmed her suspicions.

"She's got short, dark hair and a great smile. Every time she looks at him, my brother gets this goofy, sappy look on his face." Todd grimaced. "It's pretty nauseating if you think about it."

"It is not. Tell me more."

"Her name is Nancy. She's always laughing."

"There's got to be more than that." Binky considered romance her specialty.

"She's kind and compassionate. You can tell by just talking to her."

Now that he was discussing Mike and Nancy, Todd seemed less inclined to leave. He obviously liked Nancy too; it was apparent when he spoke about this new woman in his brother's life.

"Nancy is a pediatric nurse at the hospital," he added. "She works with newborns."

"Ooooh, that's interesting," Binky chirped. "She gets to be with all those little tiny babies?"

"That's her specialty. Nancy says she loves watching those babies begin to grow."

"She sounds sweet." Binky crossed her arms over her skinny waist. "I like her already and I haven't even met her yet."

"She does sound nice, Todd," Lexi agreed. "I'm happy for Mike."

"Me too," Todd said. "He's been lonely. I think it's serious for Mike this time. Just think, my big brother is in love."

"How can you tell?" Egg asked. "Mike never talks. I've been at the garage with you when I haven't heard him say more than ten or fifteen words."

"Mike is a different person now!"

"I just *knew* this was going to be a romantic story!" Binky exclaimed.

"He talks all the time now—about Nancy."

"Silent Mike? That's hard to believe!"

"It's weird for me to get used to it too. Mike's always just talked about cars. Now he tells me everything Nancy's said or done. Yesterday he informed me that even though roses are expensive, it is important for a guy to send a girl flowers—occasionally, anyway."

Lexi gave Todd a gentle nudge. "You'd better start listening to that brother of yours."

"Yeah, it's been ages since you've given Lexi a rose." Binky looked accusingly at Todd.

Todd shrugged helplessly and glanced at Egg over the top of Binky's head. "They're ganging up on me. What do I do?"

"You're a smart guy. Figure it out. I'm glad Angie isn't here to see what's going on. She might think she needed roses too." Egg was referring to Angela Hardy, the girl he had recently started dating.

"You could send your *sister* a rose." Binky batted her eyelashes in Egg's direction.

Egg ignored her.

"I'm still trying to imagine Mike being talkative," Lexi commented.

"Come to the garage and see what I mean. Mike said he'd be back about five-thirty. Why don't you stop by then?" Todd took one last look in his locker. "If I've forgotten something, I'll get it tomorrow. See you guys later." He dodged through the hallway traffic and was gone.

Binky sighed dramatically as she leaned against the locker. "Mike Winston is in love, and it's turned him into a chatterbox. What do you think about that?"

"I think there are enough chatterboxes in Cedar River," Egg said, glaring pointedly at Binky.

"Oh, chill out," Binky retorted, undisturbed by her brother's scolding.

"Are you two fighting again?" Angela Hardy joined them.

"It's nothing that we haven't heard a dozen times before," Lexi said with a laugh.

"Want to go to the Shack with us, Angie?" Egg asked.

"I can't. I promised to help Will at the mission tonight."

When Lexi and her friends had first met Angela, she was living with her mother in a welfare hotel near the Cedar River Mission. Now Angela's mother, with some help from Lexi's father and a few other friends, had found a full-time job and was taking night classes at the community college. She and her mother lived in an apartment not far from the school, but Angela often returned to the mission to answer phones, write letters, or do whatever Will Adams, the director, asked her to do.

"Work, work, work. All you do is work," Egg complained.

"I know. I'd rather not go down there tonight, but Will really needs some letters typed to be sent out in the morning. I promised I'd do it. I'm a much faster typist than he is. His 'hunt and peck' method of typing takes forever." Angela gave a cheery wave and headed down the hall.

"I guess that means it's just us," Egg commented. "Are you ready to go, Lexi?"

Lexi glanced at her watch. "I can stop at the Shack if I finish some of my homework there. I've got tons of it tonight. Remember, Todd wants me to stop at the garage too."

"It's okay," Binky said. "We can do our work together. In fact, I have some questions from our last class that I really need answered."

"Translation: Binky wants to copy your homework, Lexi. Don't let her do it."

"That's not true, Egg McNaughton!" Binky exclaimed. "Besides, I'm tons smarter than you are. . . ."

"Not!"

"Am too . . ."

They were off and running in the constant, cheerful bickering they loved so much. Lexi shook her head and picked her books out of her locker. If anyone else were to say something negative about Egg, Binky would fly into a defensive rage. But Binky felt perfectly free to scold her brother about his defects any time or place.

Egg and Binky were still debating who was most intelligent as the threesome walked through the doors of the Cedar River High School and into the parking lot.

Chapter Two

Lexi, Egg, and Binky arrived at the Hamburger Shack with the rest of the Cedar River High after-school crowd. The Shack was popular because it was close to the school and prices were low. Even Egg and Binky, who always had limited funds, could afford to stop there once or twice a week.

Jerry Randall was already behind the counter taking orders. He'd worked at the Hamburger Shack as long as Lexi had known him. Jerry was one of the first people Lexi'd met when she moved to Cedar River. That seemed like ages ago now, as Lexi looked around the room filled with her friends.

When she'd first come to Cedar River, she was lonely and timid. Now, Cedar River felt like home. Matt Windsor and Anna Marie Arnold waved from a large table on the far side of the room.

"Let's join them," Lexi pointed in their direction.

"Matt has sure turned into a teddy bear, hasn't he?" Binky commented.

Matt had been an intimidating force when Lexi first met him—sullen, brooding, angry. Now he smiled most of the time, and his dark hair and eyes didn't look the least bit forbidding.

Anna Marie had changed too. She'd gone from

15

plump to dangerously thin while she'd battled ano-
rexia. Currently she seemed to be striking a happy
medium. No longer skeleton thin, she was also not
as heavy as she'd once been.

Anna Marie patted the chair beside her. "Sit
down, Lexi. Tell me about your life. I haven't talked
to you for ages."

"There's not much to tell," Lexi sighed. "School,
study, sleep, school, study, sleep, school, study, study,
study. You know the routine."

"Do I ever." Anna Marie rolled her eyes. "What
did you think of that chemistry test we had yesterday?"

"I studied until I thought my eyes would fall out,
but when I took it, everything looked like Greek to
me. I hope I did all right."

"You always do, Lexi," Egg assured her. "No
sweat. You'll get an *A* for sure."

"*I'm* not so sure about that."

"Oh, Lexi always says that. Don't pay any attention to her," Binky interjected. "You smart people
have no self-confidence. You don't even realize how
much you know. That's why you worry about tests.
Now, if you were like me, and *knew* how much you
didn't know, it would be a different story entirely."

"*You* don't look worried about your score on the
chemistry test," Lexi pointed out.

"Why worry? I'm going to get the same grade
whether I worry or not. Besides, tests *always* look
like Greek to me, and I usually get by."

"Hmph." A guttural sound from behind Binky
made her jump.

"Jennifer Golden, I didn't see you standing
there!" Binky exclaimed.

"I was eavesdropping," Jennifer admitted. "I can't believe you guys are complaining about chemistry. What's this junk about it all being Greek to you? You should have dyslexia and *then* try to figure out a chemical equation."

Jennifer was bright and worked very hard, but her disability made reading and writing very difficult.

"You're right, Jennifer," Lexi said. "We really don't have anything to complain about. How do you think you did on the chemistry test?"

"Grim. Really grim." Jennifer morosely sank into the seat beside Matt. "I have it all learned up here," she pointed to her forehead, "but when I have to write it down, it gets jumbled up. Fortunately, the teacher understands and is really great about it. If I didn't score very well on this test, he said I could take the exam verbally tomorrow."

"Poor girl," Binky said sympathetically as she spread her books on the table to begin her homework. "It's bad enough knowing you have to take a test once, but thinking you might have to take it twice— Bleh!"

"Excuse me for changing the subject, but did any of you see the outfit that Minda Hannaford was wearing today?" Anna Marie asked.

"I did," Matt said with a grin.

"You would. That's because the skirt was so short."

"Was the skirt short?" Matt asked innocently. "I didn't notice."

"Very funny. I have handkerchiefs that are longer than that skirt."

"She was wearing tights and boots underneath

it," Lexi pointed out in Minda's defense. "And a big sweater too."

"I'm not sure why she even bothered with the skirt," Jennifer said sourly.

"It looked good on Minda," Lexi pointed out. "She has nice long legs."

"Speaking of Minda, guess who just walked though the door."

They all looked up to see Minda Hannaford and her friends, Tressa and Gina Williams, saunter into the Hamburger Shack. All three girls looked as though they'd just finished a modeling shoot for the cover of a teen magazine.

Minda's tights, miniskirt, and oversized sweater were a deep olive green. She wore a ruby turtleneck beneath the sweater and bright ruby lipstick on her pouting lips.

"Whether you like her or not," Anna Marie said, "you'll have to admit that she looks great."

"She should. She writes the fashion column for the *Cedar River Review*."

"And spends a bundle on her clothes."

"She's too much into clothing fads for my taste," Jennifer grumbled. Jennifer's usual attire—a sweatshirt and jeans—perfectly described her laid-back personality.

"Jealous?" Egg teased. "I bet you'd like to have that outfit for yourself."

"Stuff a sock in it, McNaughton," Jennifer retorted, tossing a balled-up napkin in his direction.

Anna Marie glanced around. "Where's Peggy? I thought she'd be with you after school."

"Peggy had a meeting with the coach tonight,"

Lexi explained. "She's thinking of going out for volleyball this season."

"With her height, she'd be good at spiking those balls over the net," Binky said. "But if she joins, we'll hardly see her until the season is over. She'll be at practice all the time."

"I think it would be good for her," Lexi said. "She needs to be busy."

Peggy'd had a rough year with the suicide death of her boyfriend and an unwanted pregnancy. Lexi knew it was good that Peggy was finally returning to high-school life and not spending so much time dwelling on the past.

"If she makes the team, we'll have to go and cheer her on," Lexi said aloud.

"Of course we will!" Egg liked sports of every kind.

Matt pushed away from the table. "Gotta go. Anybody need a ride home? I've got a car today instead of my motorcycle."

"I'll take one," Anna Marie said. "I've got so many books that I feel like a weight lifter."

Jennifer moved into the chair Anna Marie had just vacated. "What are the rest of us going to do?"

"Go home and study?" Egg suggested.

"Not a chance."

"Any other suggestions?"

"I'm going to the garage to talk to Todd." Lexi looked up from her notebook. "Since he claims Mike is head-over-heels in love, I have to check it out."

"Mike, ga-ga over a girl?" Jennifer exclaimed. "This I've got to see. We'll go with you."

When Lexi and Binky had finished their assignments, Egg and Jennifer walked with them to the garage. The place was in a state of chaos.

Mike Winston was normally orderly and efficient. Today, however, cars were parked helter-skelter both inside the building and out. There were tools and parts lying everywhere. Mike's desk was stacked high with bills and papers. Notes were blowing around, caught in the breeze of a small fan on the window sill.

"What's going on here?" Egg asked. "This doesn't look like the same place."

"What'd I tell you?" Todd sauntered up to his friends. Isn't this a mess?" He'd changed into jeans and a T-shirt with the sleeves rolled three times. There were grease stains and dust marks smeared across his shirt, nose, and one cheek.

"It looks as though a hurricane hit," Binky commented.

"We wouldn't have had much more confusion if a hurricane *had* blown through this place. There's work to be done everywhere. Did you see the cars lined up outside?" Todd looked thoroughly disgusted with the situation.

"When are you going to get to those?"

"Who knows? I don't even know what Mike's told his customers. He usually only makes as many appointments in the day as he can handle. He must think he's 'super mechanic' lately because he's taken on a lot more business than we can finish in a reasonable amount of time."

"This doesn't even look like Mike's place," Binky commented. "It's such a mess."

"What happened to my orderly, methodical brother?" Todd wondered aloud. "He's fallen in love and it's scrambled his brain."

"If that's what happens when you fall in love," Egg said, "then we must be very careful that it never happens to us, Todd. We can't afford to have our brains scrambled."

"I don't think you have to worry. Your brain is an omelette already," Binky muttered.

Todd stepped into the office and glared at Mike's desk. "Look at this!" He picked up a wrench. "Tools aren't supposed to be in the office. They're supposed to be on the rack on the wall. Mike picks things up and carries them around, wandering all over the garage like he's in a daze. He leaves bills in the engines and tools on the desk."

"Why are you so upset?" Binky asked. "It's not your garage."

"He's my brother. I'd hate to see him lose business—especially when I'm working for him. I don't want him to bring me down too."

"Oh, Todd, I think you're exaggerating." Lexi thought the whole situation was rather funny. Shy, orderly Mike had fallen head-over-heels in love. For the first time ever, he didn't care what the garage looked like. Apparently, no one in his family was prepared to accept the change.

"All I'm doing is running from one job to another, not knowing where to begin. Mike didn't even prioritize these work orders." Todd scowled at the mess on the desk.

"What's wrong with you, little brother? Lighten up." Mike Winston's voice from across the room caught Todd by surprise. He turned to see his brother framed in the doorway of the shop.

"You haven't learned the first thing about work yet, have you?" Mike sauntered into the building. He was a darker, taller version of Todd. "There's always work to be done, and it never goes away, so you might as well have a little fun on the side, right?"

"I can't believe that's coming out of *his* mouth," Todd muttered. "That's a lot different than the 'you-can't-go-home-until-all-your-work-is-done' lecture I usually get."

Mike grinned widely at all of them. He seemed unaware of the mess. "Hi, Lexi. Hi, Egg, Binky, Jennifer. What's happening?"

In all the time Lexi had known Mike, she'd rarely received more than a shy smile and a nod when she'd come into the shop. Today, Mike treated them like long lost friends.

"So, tell me," he said. "How's school?"

"You don't want to know," Jennifer said morosely. "Chemistry is so impossible."

"I always hated chemistry too," Mike sympathized. "But don't let it get you down. Just hang in there."

"The Emerald Tones are doing all right," Binky volunteered. "We've been trying to talk Mrs. Waverly into letting us do another tour, but so far, she hasn't succumbed to our pressure."

"Would *you* want to get on a bus with dozens of high-school kids, travel around the country, and try to make them sing when they'd rather goof off?" Mike asked.

"Ooooh, I guess you're right." Binky made a face. "Maybe there is a good reason she doesn't want to do another tour for a while. The poor woman probably needs a rest."

"Hey, Egg. Where's Angela?" Mike asked.

Egg's eyebrows flew upward. He was obviously

surprised that Mike knew the name of his girlfriend.

"Angie? Huh, um, uh," Egg stuttered. "She's fine. Great. She's working at the mission tonight. She does that a lot. I don't get to see her very much. She and her mom have a real hang-up about work. The guy at the mission says they have a fear of being homeless again. They figure that if they work as hard as they can, all the time, they can prevent that. I wish she had more free time for dates."

Binky poked her brother in the arm. "What are you complaining about? You never have enough money to go out on dates anyway. You should be glad you like a girl who doesn't care whether you go out or not."

"Think of how much money you're saving," Jennifer teased.

"There's more to dating than just spending money, you know. We like to spend time together too."

"Holding hands and looking into each other's eyes," Binky sneered. "They are so sappy."

Egg blushed red from the base of his neck to his hairline.

"Leave your brother alone. There's nothing wrong with holding hands and looking sappy." Mike's grin widened.

"This is the guy who should know," Todd added. Mike began to blush just as intensely as Egg.

Lexi watched the entire exchange in amazement. Mike's personality had done a complete flip-flop. As long as she'd known the brothers, Mike had stayed in the background. Todd was the outgoing and friendly one. Now Mike had found center stage.

To change the subject, Mike began a rapid-fire

series of crazy jokes that had the kids laughing so hard that Binky was holding her sides and groaning. They were all startled when a loud horn honked right behind them.

Lexi jumped and Binky squealed.

"Whoops. Sorry about that," Mike said, still chuckling. "I forgot I had a customer coming in for an oil change. That's him now."

Mike sauntered to the door to visit with the man whose car was blocking the doorway. To every request the customer had, Lexi heard Mike say, "Sure, no problem. We'll take care of it."

After the man turned the keys over to Mike and left the garage, Todd said, "You told him we were too busy, I hope."

"Get off my back," Mike retorted carelessly. "It's no big deal. Oil change, tires rotated. All that maintenance stuff. We'll get it done."

"When did you tell him he could pick it up?"

"Tomorrow morning on his way to work."

"Tomorrow morning!" Todd didn't even attempt to keep his voice down or his temper in check. "Are you nuts? We can't have that car ready by tomorrow! Look at this place. Look at all the job orders we have. There are two dozen people ahead of him. You've always said, 'first come, first served,' Mike. There are work orders here dated three and four days ago. What's wrong with you?"

Lexi and Egg exchanged a worried glance. Neither of them had ever seen Todd and his brother fight. Binky and Jennifer shifted awkwardly from one foot to the other, not quite sure if they should leave quietly or stay to listen.

"You've been promising too much, Mike. We can't

get this all done. Not only have you overcommitted yourself, you're not in the shop to do the work. I'm not a mechanic. *You* are. I can't hold this place together after school while you go off romancing Nancy."

"Chill out, little brother. We'll get it all done. Don't worry. Nancy's working tonight. I'll stay here all night if I have to."

"That's our problem, Mike. You only want to work when Nancy's busy. When she's home, you just skip out of the garage like it's a Sunday picnic."

"When did you become my father?" Mike barked. "It's *my* shop. It's *my* job. I'll worry about it when I'm ready."

"You've *made* it my business. You have me working here. I can't keep up. Don't you understand?"

Lexi, Egg, Binky, and Jennifer glanced at each other with worried expressions.

"Let's get out of here," Egg mouthed.

Jennifer nodded. "Now."

Chapter Three

They tiptoed quietly toward the door. Mike and Todd were so engrossed in their discussion they didn't even notice when the foursome slipped around the customer's car and out the door.

"Whew," Egg said. "I'm glad we left. I didn't want to be in the middle of that battle."

"I don't think I've ever seen Todd and Mike have a disagreement before. They usually get along so well."

"I can see Todd's point of view," Egg said. "He's getting left with a lot of work at the garage, and when he gets home he still has his homework to do."

"It's Mike's business," Jennifer pointed out. "Mike should be the one worrying about whether jobs are all getting done on time or not."

"I can see both sides," Binky said. "It's just like my problems with Egg."

"You don't have any problems with me."

"Sure I do. I get upset with you if you don't have your schoolwork done on time because I don't want to see you fail at something and embarrass yourself." Binky paused for a moment before adding, "And me."

"How could *my* failure embarrass you?" Egg asked.

"You're part of my family," Binky said. "Although we don't always agree, we are pretty close."

"Don't *always* agree?" Jennifer blurted. "You two *never* agree."

Binky and Egg both turned to stare at Jennifer with dumbfounded looks on their faces. "What are you talking about?" they asked in unison.

"All the fighting and bickering you do! All the disagreements you have!"

Binky and Egg shook their heads simultaneously. "We don't fight."

"Hardly ever."

"And especially not about little things."

"Jennifer, you don't know what you're talking about."

Now it was Jennifer's turn to look astounded. "You mean you don't think you ever argue?"

"Never," they said as one voice.

Jennifer turned to Lexi and threw her hands in the air. "I can't believe I heard that with my own ears. Binky and Egg don't think they fight."

Lexi burst out laughing. "They're just doing what they've always done. That's how they communicate."

"I'd say we're communicating pretty well compared to Todd and Mike right now."

"Which worries me." Lexi's step slowed. "Maybe I should go back and talk to them."

"What can you do?" Jennifer asked.

"I don't know. Maybe nothing—but I feel like I should try."

"Sorry I can't stay to help, but I've got to get home," Jennifer said.

"We do too," Binky rejoined.

"Go on. I'll run back for a minute and talk to

Todd." Lexi waved her friends away and returned to the garage.

She was surprised to find Todd there alone, tinkering with something under the hood of a car. Mike had disappeared. Todd had a fresh grease stain on his shirt and a grim expression on his face.

"Where'd he go?" Lexi blurted.

"Who knows? To Nancy's house, or to the hospital where Nancy works, or to order flowers for Nancy, or to buy something for Nancy. Everything my brother does these days is motivated by Nancy."

"Worse things could have happened to him," Lexi reminded Todd gently.

"I suppose that's true, but this is really irritating. Mike has changed so much I hardly recognize him sometimes."

"He's fallen head-over-heels in love. He doesn't know which end is up anymore."

Todd didn't laugh. "It might be funny to everyone else, but it's not funny to me. Mike's not paying attention to this business. Pretty soon his steady customers are going to leave him." Todd waved his arm toward the clutter and congestion. "I'm just a kid who comes down here to help after school and on weekends. I shouldn't be left with this mess."

"You'll have to talk to your brother about it when he's not so . . . giddy."

"Nancy's a great girl, Lexi. But it seems my brother's forgotten about everything else that was important to him now that she's come into his life."

Todd sank onto a low stool. "It's going to take a miracle to straighten this shop out again."

The bell above the shop's door jingled, and a tall, thin man with a wide grin and sandy brown hair walked through the entrance. He wore clean but faded jeans and a well-washed plaid cotton shirt. His haircut appeared to have been done with a butcher knife or a lawn mower. It stuck up in curly clumps and bunches all over his head. He had obviously tried to tame the mop. His hair was still damp, and there were comb tracks through the thick brown curls. The guy looked pleasant, sweet-natured, and as nervous as any human being Lexi had ever seen before.

"I . . . uh . . . I . . . I'm Ed Bell," he stammered.

Todd stood up and moved to shake his hand. "Hi, I'm Todd Winston, and this is Lexi Leighton. Can we help you?"

Lexi could see Todd peering over Mr. Bell's shoulder toward the driveway. She could almost read Todd's mind—*Please, don't bring me another car job today. I can't handle it.*

"If you have some car work that needs to be done," Todd began, "I'm afraid that I won't be able to tackle it tonight. My brother is the mechanic, and he's out of the shop right now."

Mr. Bell shook his head. "Oh, no, that's not it at all. I don't have a car to repair."

"Then what can I do for you?"

Ed, who appeared to be in his midthirties, shifted uncomfortably from one foot to the other. "I suppose I shouldn't have just walked in off the street like this, but, the fact is, I need a job."

Before Todd could say anything, Mr. Bell rushed on. "I'm good with my hands. I can fix most any car on the road today." He glanced around the shop at the clutter and confusion. "I hope you don't mind my saying so, but it looks like you could use a little help in here. We could have most of these cars fixed and out of here within forty-eight hours."

Ed looked as though he were ready to roll up his sleeves and start working. Lexi suppressed a smile. She'd liked Ed the moment she saw him. He reminded her a little of what Egg might be like as a grown man. He was tall and lanky with big joints that made him move like a scarecrow. And she loved his eyes. They were bright blue and twinkled merrily.

"I can't tell you how much I'd like to have you start working right this minute," Todd said. "But, Mr. Bell . . ."

"Call me Ed," the man insisted. "No one ever calls me Mr. Bell. I wouldn't know how to respond."

"Well, Ed," Todd began again. "As I said, my brother owns this shop, and he'd probably be upset if he came back to find that I'd hired a mechanic without consulting him." Todd moved toward Mike's cluttered desk and pawed through the papers on top of it. Finally, in a bottom drawer, he found what he was looking for.

"Here's a job application form. Why don't you fill it out and bring it back when my brother's around? He's usually here early in the morning."

Todd handed Ed the one-page application form. Lexi was surprised at the flicker of apprehension that crossed Ed's face.

"In fact," Todd went on, "why don't you just sit down at Mike's desk and fill out the form right now? I can give it to my brother to look over tonight. You could come back in the morning to talk to him."

Ed took a step backward. "No, uh, no. I don't think so."

"It would be really helpful to Mike if he had a little time to study your application," Todd suggested.

"I don't have time to fill it out right now. I'm sorry. I hope that's okay. If it's not, well, I guess I'm just out of luck."

"Then just fill it out tonight and bring it back tomorrow when Mike's around."

Ed's head bounced in agreement. "That would be best. Definitely best." He clutched the application form to his chest and backed toward the door. "Thanks a lot for your help. I really appreciate it. I'm glad I met you. Thank you. Thanks very much. Thanks a lot. Bye." He was still thanking them when he disappeared around the corner of the door.

Lexi and Todd burst out laughing.

"What a sweet, funny guy," Lexi commented.

"He was, wasn't he? You know, he reminded me of someone, but I can't put my finger on who it might be."

Lexi giggled. "Does Egg 'Edward' McNaughton come to mind?"

"That's it! Ed Bell is like a grown-up Egg. No wonder I liked him so much. Wouldn't it be great if he were just the kind of mechanic Mike needed around here?"

"He certainly appeared eager to work."

"That's what we want." Todd put his hands on his hips and stared around the shop. "It's pretty amazing that Ed walked through that door just when we were talking about how much we needed help."

"You *did* say that getting this place back in order

was going to take a miracle."

Todd grinned and looked out the door and into the street. "Yeah, I did say that. I wonder if Mr. Ed Bell's middle name is Miracle?"

Chapter Four

"Here, Lexi. Use this color for your trees." Benjamin thrust a bright pink crayon under Lexi's nose. It was late Saturday afternoon, and Lexi and her brother, Ben, were entertaining themselves with Ben's coloring books.

"I don't want my trees to be pink, Ben. I think I'm going to make them purple."

Ben wrinkled his nose. "Who ever heard of purple trees?" Lexi grinned and ruffled her little brother's hair. "That's the good thing about coloring, Ben. You can make your picture any color that you want."

"Then I'm going to make this puppy orange."

Lexi's mother burst out laughing as she stood at the counter peeling carrots. "You two have the strangest conversations!" she exclaimed. "I don't know who is more of a child, Lexi, you or Ben."

"I'm not a child," Ben assured his mother. "I'm a big kid."

"So, big kid," Lexi said, "tell me about your week at the Academy. Did you learn anything?"

"We learned that the janitor's face turns red when somebody pours milk in the garbage can."

"That's a real academic accomplishment."

"And we learned you can't go outside when the bell doesn't ring."

"Two good things to know." Lexi suppressed a giggle. "Did you learn anything about letters or numbers or words?"

Ben screwed his face into a thoughtful frown. "No. Don't think so."

"Mom, are you sure you're getting your money's worth out of the Academy?" Lexi teased. There was laughter in her voice. Ben's school, the Academy for the Handicapped, was considered one of the finest in the area.

"Ben, I think you're not telling us something. Didn't I hear from your teacher that you could count all the way to thirty?"

"I can, I can. One . . . two . . . three . . ."

Ben's recital was cut short by the ring of the telephone. Mrs. Leighton reached for the phone.

"It's for you, Lexi."

Lexi glanced at her little brother. He'd begun to sing the alphabet song. "I'll take it in the other room, Mom."

She hurried into the living room to pick up the receiver. "Lexi, it's Todd."

"Hi. What's up?"

"I'm calling from the shop."

"Are things any better there?" Lexi asked hopefully.

"A little. Mike worked late and also came back to work about six A.M. this morning. He got quite a few things done. At least we don't have customers standing in the doorway yelling for their vehicles."

"Why are you calling if you're so busy?" Lexi wondered aloud.

"Because I wanted to invite you to go out for dinner with me tonight. Mike suggested it. He'd like you and Nancy to meet."

"That's really nice, Todd. Tell Mike thanks."

"Maybe you won't *want* to thank him after you see what a bowl of jelly Mike has turned into. He just loses it when he's around Nancy."

"I think you're exaggerating."

"You'll have to see for yourself. Wait until tonight."

"Just a minute. I'll go check with Mom."

When Lexi returned to the phone, she was smiling. "She thinks it's a great idea."

"We'll pick you up in an hour. Is that enough time to get ready?"

"Sure. See you then." Lexi hung up the phone and smiled into the mirror over the mantel. This was going to be fun. She'd always liked Todd's brother Mike, but because he was so shy, she didn't know him very well. This would be a wonderful opportunity to get to know both Mike and his girlfriend.

"Are you going to color anymore, Lexi?" Ben hollered from the kitchen.

Lexi poked her head through the kitchen door. "I can't, Ben. I'm going out for dinner. I have to get ready."

"You look ready to me."

"I have to get in the shower and do my hair. I think I'll paint my fingernails." She waggled a finger under Ben's nose. "I have lots to do."

After her shower, Lexi blow-dried her hair while standing in front of the open door to her closet. There was a rap on her door and Lexi's mother stepped into the room. "Trying to pick out something to wear?"

"I think I'd better quit sewing. My closet is getting jam-packed. I can't even see my choices anymore. Everything is just stuffed inside."

"How about this one?" Lexi's mother pulled out a sleeveless black dress with white polka dots. "Or maybe this," and she pulled out a teal pleated skirt and an oversized sweater.

"Maybe the skirt and sweater," Lexi said. "That's a little less formal. Todd didn't say where we were going. But, we're probably eating on a limited budget." Lexi slipped into the clothes her mother had chosen.

"It was nice of Mike to invite me. Todd's been complaining about both Mike and Nancy the last few days. I'll be glad to meet Nancy and see what she's *really* like."

"I'm sure she's lovely," Mrs. Leighton said. "It seems the Winston boys have good taste in girls."

Lexi grinned at her mother but didn't comment because the doorbell rang at that moment.

Lexi gave her mother a kiss on the cheek and started down the stairs. Todd was waiting in the foyer wearing dark pants and a white shirt. He'd even put on a tie.

Lexi gave a long, low whistle. "Don't you look great!"

Todd poked his finger into the knot of his tie. "Mike made me dress up. He always wants everything to be perfect for Nancy. I feel like a waiter."

"Don't be silly. You look wonderful."

"You'll have to remind me not to take your order once we get to the restaurant," Todd said sarcastically.

"I think it's sweet."

"Wearing this tie doesn't feel so sweet. I think I'm being strangled."

"Oh, quit being such a grump. Where are Mike and Nancy? In the car?"

"No, we're meeting them at the restaurant. Mike wanted to be 'alone' with Nancy. He said he had something important to discuss with her."

"Sounds like he wanted her all to himself."

"You've got that right."

When they'd settled themselves in Todd's car, Lexi leaned her head against the back of the seat and said, "Tell me all about Nancy. I'd like to have some idea of what she's like before I meet her."

"She's an athlete. She plays softball and tennis during the summer and racquetball in the winter."

"Impressive."

"And, she's the best thing that's ever happened to my brother Mike."

"I can hardly believe I'm hearing that from you," Lexi said. "You're the one who's been mad at Mike lately!"

"Oh, that's Mike's fault, not Nancy's," Todd assured her. "She can't control the fact that my brother acts like a big goofball when he's in love." Todd pulled into the restaurant parking lot, and Lexi gave a little gasp of surprise.

"The Wok! I've never eaten here before."

"I hope you like Chinese food. Nancy suggested it."

The restaurant was low-slung with many windows across the face of the building. At the entrance, there were large pillars and a shiny gold fire-breathing dragon. Inside, exotic oriental music played softly, and Lexi could hear the sound of a stream running.

"This is great," she looked around. "Hey, there

are trees growing inside this restaurant!"

Todd looked up at the skylights. "Nancy thought we'd like it."

"May I help you?" The hostess, a delicate woman in a kimono, greeted them.

"We're here to meet another couple. Mike Winston." The lady's head bobbed. "Yes, yes, they've already arrived. Just follow me."

She led them through a maze of tables and across a small bridge under which ran a stream. Mike and Nancy were seated in a cozy corner away from the other restaurant traffic.

"See? They wanted to be alone together even here," Todd muttered. "Can you believe it?"

When they neared the table, Mike jumped to his feet. "Hi. Glad you found us. We just got here a few minutes ago." He looked affectionately at the woman across the table from him. "Nancy, this is Todd's friend, Lexi Leighton. Lexi, I'd like you to meet Nancy Kelvin."

Nancy was athletic-looking, just as Todd had said. She had short dark hair and eyes that danced when she smiled. Nancy was just a little taller than Lexi, but her well-toned body, square shoulders, and firm handshake made Lexi feel like a twig.

"It's about time we met, Lexi," Nancy said. "I've been hearing about you from Todd, Mike, and Mr. and Mrs. Winston. I told Mike that if I didn't meet you soon, I was going to think they'd made you up! But here you are. I'm glad to see you."

"Thanks." Nancy's friendliness was contagious. "I've been hearing a lot about you too."

Nancy gave Todd a sly look. "Complaints, probably. I know that Mike hasn't been spending enough time at the shop lately, and I'm afraid it's my fault." She turned toward Mike and lowered her eyelashes at him. "But I really can't help it. I love to have him with me."

"Here we go again," Todd murmured. "Mike, if you don't quit looking at Nancy like a lovesick calf, none of us are going to be able to eat dinner. We'll all be too nauseated." Then Todd turned to Nancy. "I'm sorry, but it's just too much for me to handle. My brother's never been the romantic type until now. It's taking some getting used to."

Nancy sat down and put her hand over Mike's. "I'm glad to hear that Mike doesn't fall in love easily. *That* would make me worry."

It became even more obvious during the course of the meal how very much in love Mike and Nancy were. It was apparent in the looks they exchanged, the way he held her hand across the table, and the way he fussed over her.

"If you don't like your dinner," Mike offered when the food arrived, "I'll trade you my steak for that shrimp. It looks kind of small. Are you sure it'll be enough for you?"

"I'm fine, Mike. This is exactly what I ordered. Besides, who wants to eat steak in a Chinese restaurant anyway, except you?"

"I suppose I could have ordered chow mein or something." Mike stared at his plate.

"Nancy, you could talk him into eating his shoes with a little salt and pepper," Todd pointed out. "I'm not sure what kind of power you have over him, but I wish you could bottle it. I'd take some."

"It would take more than bottled charm to get me to listen to you, little brother," Mike teased.

As the brothers bantered, Nancy joined right in. It seemed as though they were already one family.

"So, tell me, Lexi, how's school?" Nancy asked.

"All right, I guess." Lexi wrinkled her nose. "School is school."

Nancy nodded sympathetically. "I never liked it much when I was in high school, either. It seemed so slow and boring. College is better, though. And once you get out into the work force and begin doing what you've been trained to do, it's great."

Lexi admired Nancy's natural forthright manner. She could understand why the Winstons liked her so much.

"Todd said you work at the hospital."

"I'm a pediatric nurse. I get to take care of those beautiful little newborn babies." Nancy's eyes began to sparkle. "They are such perfect little miracles that it's a real honor to be able to work with them every day."

"Do you ever care for any really tiny babies?"

"Preemies, you mean? The little guys that are only a couple pounds when they're born? Oh, sure. I like them a lot. Those babies are real scrappers. They have to fight for their lives, and they do. Even when they're only a few hours old, they know how important it is that they use every ounce of energy for growing and staying well. I love *all* children, as you might have guessed, but I love the little guys the most of all. Aren't I lucky to have a job that makes me so happy?"

Mike looked up from his plate long enough to give Nancy an adoring smile.

"I've talked about myself enough," Nancy said. "We should talk about you."

Lexi told them about Ben and his experiences at the Academy. She mentioned her mother's painting and her father's veterinary clinic. Nancy listened with rapt interest.

"That's great," Nancy exclaimed. "You and I are going to have lots of fun getting to know each other, aren't we, Lexi?"

At that moment, Mike cleared his throat. "Ahem . . . ahem. Would you two mind letting me get a word in edgewise here?"

"Well, I don't know," Nancy teased. "Talk me into it."

"How about if I told you that I had some good news to announce? This probably won't come as any big surprise to Todd and Lexi, but I hired someone today to help me in the shop."

"Wonderful!" Nancy exclaimed. "Now you won't feel guilty about being away from the business for more than two minutes at a time."

"I *had* let things get a little out of hand," Mike admitted. "But it seemed like, once I met you . . ." his voice trailed away.

"Who'd you hire, Mike?" Todd pulled on the sleeve of his brother's shirt.

"His name is Ed Bell. He said he talked to you the first time he came into the shop."

"Oh, that's great!" Lexi exclaimed happily. "I really liked him."

"He liked you too. Best of all, if Ed and I can get caught up, we should be in pretty good shape for the rest of the winter."

"You've needed help for a long time," Todd said. "I'm glad you got Ed. He seems like a great guy."

"This is a special night," Nancy concluded. "We

need to celebrate." She flung her hand in the air and signaled a waiter to come over. "Sir," she said, "we need to see the dessert tray immediately."

"Dessert?" Mike moaned. "I'm so full I can hardly sit straight."

"Nonsense," Nancy said with a shake of her head. "When good things happen, celebrate. Take advantage of every opportunity."

Lexi and Nancy looked at each other across the table and grinned. Lexi could tell she was going to like her new friend.

Chapter Five

The Madison house was filled with laughter and noise as Peggy and her friends gathered to study.

"Binky, is there any pepperoni pizza left?" Egg peered across the littered table.

"This is sausage. Will that do?"

Egg's expectant look vanished. "I wanted pepperoni."

"You ate seven pieces of pizza, Egg. Aren't you full?" Jennifer asked.

"That's one amazing thing about my brother." Binky pushed the plate toward Egg. "He *never* gets full."

"Where do you put it?" Lexi mused. "You're as skinny as a stick and you eat like a horse."

Todd picked up the pizza cutter and sliced off another piece of the sausage pizza. "Leave him alone. Egg needs his strength. He's a growing boy. He has to eat."

"Why are you defending Egg?" Jennifer asked. "He's your main competition for the pizza."

Todd leaned back in his chair with a satisfied grin. "I'm mellow today. I've got the day off."

"It *has* been a while since you studied with us," Peggy agreed, tugging at the bow holding back her hair. "I thought Mike had you chained to some old car body in the shop and wouldn't let you go."

"It's felt that way. But ever since Mike hired a new mechanic, the whole place has turned around. I don't know how we managed to get along without Ed Bell as long as we did."

Egg reached across the table for a piece of licorice. "I said hello to him last night when I was at the shop looking for you. He's a pretty good-looking guy, isn't he?"

Lexi and Todd burst into laughter.

"What's so funny?"

"Todd and I both said that Ed reminded us of you! Now, here you are, telling us what a *good-looking* guy he is."

"Well, he *is* good-looking. And he's probably smart, too." Egg grinned. "Just like me, right?"

"Ed is like having a whirlwind working in the shop," Todd said. "He comes in early and stays late. He works harder than any other guy I've ever seen. He's done more repair jobs in the last two days than we'd gotten done in the last two weeks!"

"He sounds too good to be true," Jennifer commented.

"Oh, he's not perfect. There are some things about him that drive Mike absolutely crazy.

"For example, he refuses to do the billing or paper work on any of the cars. He just hands it to me or Mike and says, 'I don't like doing that stuff. You do it. I'll fix cars.' Mike is always chasing after him with a clipboard in his hand asking him what he's done to this car or that. Every time Mike tells him to pick up a pencil and fill out the forms himself, Ed just says that it's a waste of his time. 'I hate paperwork,' he says, 'You're good at it. You do it.'

"I thought for sure that Mike would get mad and tell him to do it himself, but Ed is so efficient with the cars that Mike's decided it's easier not to argue about the paperwork. He's doing it himself. Mike thinks Ed might be the answer to all our problems."

"I wish I had an answer to all my problems," Egg muttered. "Like someone to make me another pepperoni pizza."

"Eat the sausage." Binky poked her brother. "It's good for you."

Todd ignored them both. "Mike told me his most hard-to-please customer was in the shop yesterday afternoon. The guy insisted on being first in line when there were several others waiting. It's a trick this customer always tries to pull, but Mike never lets him get away with it. Mike just sat back to see how Ed would handle things."

"What happened?"

"Ed managed to convince the guy that he really didn't need his car as quickly as he thought he did. To keep the customer happy, Ed made a deal. If the fellow would be patient for a few hours, Ed would throw in a car wash for free. When the customer came back to pick up his car, he was happy because he thought he'd gotten something extra for his money. Better yet, Ed had a few more hours to get the jobs ahead of this one done first."

"Ed sounds like a pretty smart guy to me," Binky commented.

"That's what Mike thinks. He's already talking about having Ed do appointment scheduling and bookwork in the office."

"I thought you said Ed didn't like that sort of thing."

"I'm sure my brother will talk him into it. The garage is a small operation. Besides, Mike is in love. He wants free time when Nancy has days off. Since her schedule is always changing at the hospital, Ed may be the answer to Mike's problems. Ed seems driven to do well in this job. If Mike asked him to stand on the roof and sing, he'd probably try it. He acts as though he has something to prove."

"Why? He's already a good mechanic."

"I don't know. I can't figure it out, but Mike's just glad to have somebody to help out at the shop."

"Maybe the guy is just a hard worker."

"Could be," Todd agreed. "But sometimes when he's doing something, he has this strange look on his face. It's almost a look of . . . pain."

"Pain?"

"It's as if he's doing something that's so hard on him that it physically hurts him."

"Weird," Binky concluded.

"There's something really intense about Ed," Todd continued.

"I hear you went out for dinner with Mike and Nancy the other night," Peggy commented. "Lexi said it was great."

Egg made big wet smooching sounds with his lips. "The lovebirds were flocking together. Isn't that sweet?"

"Do you think Mike and Nancy will get married, Todd?" Jennifer asked.

"He hasn't mentioned marriage to me yet, but, who knows?"

"I'll bet they do get married," Binky said. "Ooooh, that's so romantic. I hope we can come to the wedding. Could you introduce us to Nancy? Maybe that would help us to get an invitation."

"Binky, you're such a sap."

"No, I'm not. I love weddings. All those flowers, candles, and beautiful dresses. And I like to look at guys in tuxedos and those sweet little flower girls . . . and the singing!"

"The thing I like best about weddings is the food," Egg commented. "If only they'd make the portions bigger. Those little tiny sandwiches and cookies aren't enough. I have to go back six times to make a meal."

"My favorite part is throwing rice," Binky continued, her eyes glowing. "And I like to see if I can catch the bridal bouquet when the bride tosses it."

"What would you do if you actually caught a bouquet, Binky? Isn't the girl who catches the bridal bouquet supposed to be the next bride to walk down the aisle?"

Binky's eyes gleamed. "That *would* be romantic, wouldn't it?"

"Not when you're a junior in high school!"

"I still hope we get invited to Mike and Nancy's wedding."

Todd burst out laughing. "You've already got my brother walking down the aisle, and I don't think he's asked Nancy to marry him yet."

"Can either Mike or Nancy cook?" Binky asked.

Binky's friends stopped what they were doing to stare at her.

"Who cares if they can cook or not?"

"What does that have to do with anything?"

"It's a very important question," Binky insisted. "Cooking is a skill that not many young people have today."

Lexi knew her friend well. The strange twist this conversation had taken was a sure sign that something weird was up with Binky.

"I think it's a shame we don't learn more about cooking. After all, once we graduate from high school, we're going to have to start feeding ourselves. I don't want to have to eat *everything* out of a box or a can."

"It wouldn't bother me a bit," Egg commented. "Everything we eat is out of a box or a can right now."

"That's what the teenagers in this country lack— homemaking skills."

"I think I'm doing pretty well," Peggy defended herself. "I made the pizzas today."

"All right, Binky, what's up? We know you too well to think that this conversation is coming out of the blue."

Binky's cheeks grew pink, and she dropped her chin to her chest. "It's no big thing. Just a little contest I entered."

"You entered a cooking contest?"

"Not exactly. I was in the home economics department picking up a library book I'd left there when I saw this notice for a homemaking skills competition."

"And *you* decided to sign up?" Egg asked, horrified.

"It was a really interesting poster," Binky defended herself. "And the contest is supposed to get everyone interested in the home economics curriculum. Anybody in school can enter. There are several categories from which to choose. If you enter the bread-baking category, then you compete by bringing a sample of your home-baked bread to the contest, that's all. It doesn't sound so bad."

"I didn't think you were the domestic type," Todd commented.

"I'm not, but I decided that maybe I should be. Besides, the home ec. teacher was in the room recruiting entrants for the contest. It seemed tacky to say no to a teacher. Do you know what I mean?"

"*You* were afraid to say no, Binky?" Jennifer gasped. "That doesn't sound like you at all."

"There *was* this one other little bitty thing that made me think the contest sounded pretty interesting."

"Ah-hah! Now for the *real* reason you signed up!"

"There are going to be prizes for the winners."

"You're not entering this contest because you want to learn to be a better homemaker," Peggy deduced, "but because you want the prizes they're offering?"

"They must be great prizes," Lexi commented.

"Oh, they are, Lexi! Wonderful prizes. Do you know what the grand prize is? A trip to a water park, that new one about thirty miles from here. It's supposed to be great. Your whole family can go and spend the day. There's a lunch included."

"You'd have to be quite a little homemaker to win that prize, wouldn't you?" Todd asked.

Binky waved her hand expansively in the air. "Oh, even if I didn't get first prize, there are other good prizes too. Second prize is a boom box, just like the one I've been looking at in Allen's department store. It's got a CD player and dual cassette decks. It's absolutely perfect. If I could win that, I'd be happy."

"So, you really entered this contest for reasons of

greed, right, Binky?" Egg deduced. "And you're not actually enthusiastic about cooking or housekeeping."

"No, but I *am* interested in a trip to a water park or winning a boom box. I knew you would be too, Egg."

Egg's eyes grew round and he blinked twice. "What did you say?"

"I knew *you'd* like to take a trip to the water park too. And I know you want a boom box just as much as I do. We were both disappointed when we didn't get them for Christmas last year. That's why I signed you up for the contest too. If I don't win a prize, you will!"

Egg turned pale. "I don't want to be in any homemaking skills contest. No way. No how. No thanks. Forget it. End of subject."

"Oh, Egg, you don't mean that." Binky behaved as though Egg had not protested at all. "It's going to be great. I think you'll be a sure-fire winner. There weren't any guys signed up. Don't you realize how happy the judges will be to see a *male* contestant? They're just going to eat you up, Egg."

"No guys but me?" Egg was looking a little sick. "You go right back to the home ec. department and take my name off that list. Don't you *ever* sign me up for anything again without asking my permission first!"

"Just chill, Egg. I can't take your name off the list now. The home ec. teacher was so glad to see a boy's name on the sign-up sheet that she practically did cartwheels. Besides, I refuse to take your name off the list. It's the principle of the thing."

"Principle! What principle?"

"I don't want the contest to be sexist," Binky exclaimed. "Men have to learn how to take care of homes too. Men have to be responsible for their own lives. This is one place to start."

"I'm perfectly happy being responsible for my own life. Go find other people to make fools of themselves. Get Todd to sign up. Talk to Matt Windsor and Tim Anders. Leave me out of this!"

"It will be good for you, Egg. You need to know how to cook and sew. Once you go to college, you'll be thanking me for this."

"Binky, I won't even be speaking to you when I go to college if you don't get my name off that list."

"Egg, I *need* you to be in that contest. After all, there's just the tiniest little chance that I might not win first or second place."

"The tiniest little chance?" Jennifer muttered sarcastically. "She's pretty confident for a girl who doesn't know how to boil water."

"If I don't win first or second place, you'll have to win it for me. If I win the trip to the water park, I'll take you; if you win, you can take me."

"You're the *last* person I'm going to invite to anything, Binky McNaughton," Egg warned.

"You're just nervous right now," Binky assured her brother. "You'll feel better later. Why, Egg, we've practically got this contest in the bag. Haven't we cooked Chinese food for our friends? Anything else we try can't be harder than that."

"Aren't you the one who pulled the fortunes out of every fortune cookie and then couldn't figure out how to get them back in?" Todd reminded Binky gently.

"Oh, that." Binky tossed her head. "A technicality. It didn't matter, did it? I just handed the cookies and the fortunes out separately. You know that."

Egg was sputtering like a wet firecracker. His adam's apple bobbed up and down like a rubber ball on a wave. His face grew a deep rosy pink. He shot out of his chair like a ball out of a cannon. "Binky, we have to talk about this *in private*."

"Egg, you're making a big deal over nothing."

"Come with me, right now. Maybe we can get into the school and get my name off that list."

"Don't be silly. You don't want your name off that list. Just think of the water park. A full day—for free. Lunch and transportation is included."

They left Peggy's house with hardly a goodbye. Egg was too busy insisting that he would not be in the contest; Binky, insisting that he would. Binky's voice floated back to them as the front door closed.

"But Egg, you *have* to be in this contest. There are *prizes* to consider!"

Chapter Six

"What did you think about the argument Egg and Binky had at Peggy's last night?" Todd asked Lexi as they drove away from the school toward Mike's garage.

"It was just one more crazy, typical Egg and Binky problem. Except we usually don't see Egg *that* upset with his sister."

"Binky was more stubborn than usual, too. She absolutely insisted that Egg be in the contest."

"They'll be okay. They always are. I'm just glad that I don't live at the McNaughtons' while Egg is on domestic duty."

Todd whistled as he pulled up to the garage. "Wow, do you see that?"

Lexi looked around. "I don't see anything."

"That's what I mean. There aren't any cars in line waiting to be worked on."

"Where did they all go?"

Todd slipped the keys out of the ignition and into his pocket. All the doors and windows of the garage were open. As they stepped into the building, Lexi was struck by the scent of lemony soap and fresh air.

"What's happened to this place? It smells so . . . clean!"

"Hi, guys. How are you?" Ed rolled out from the underside of a car on a creeper and jumped nimbly to his feet. Whistling cheerfully, he walked to the front of the car and popped open the hood.

"Nice day we're having, isn't it?" he said conversationally. "Thought I'd open the doors and windows to air it out in here. Does it smell better? All those gasoline and oil fumes can get to a person after a while."

"It looks like you scrubbed this place from top to bottom, too."

"I didn't have any place to go on my noon hour, so I started doing a little cleaning," Ed admitted. "Maybe I got carried away, but I think it looks better in here."

"This place looks great. I've always thought my brother kept a pretty neat garage, but you've really fixed things up."

"All Mike needed was a little help to get caught up. We're in good shape now, so I can ease up."

"No, you can't." Mike caught them by surprise as he stepped out of his office. "You can't ease up a bit, Ed. Now that you've got this place running so smoothly, I'll be able to take more time off to spend with Nancy. You're going to be as busy as ever."

Ed and Mike grinned at each other. Mike, Lexi noticed, was much more relaxed than he had been before Ed's arrival.

Todd noticed it too. "Ed, your coming to work for my brother has been nothing short of a miracle."

"He's right. I was slacking off before Ed came along. Now we're in better shape than I've been in weeks. Our customers are happy. I'm happy. Everybody's happy!" Mike's eyes twinkled. "And Nancy will be especially happy to hear that I've got more time."

Mike glanced at his watch. "In fact, I'm going to run down the street right now and order some flowers for her before the shop closes. I know you guys can hold down the fort." With a wave, Mike jogged out the door and veered to the left toward the florist shop.

Todd moved closer to Ed to peer into the car's engine.

"Can you figure out what's wrong with this carburetor, Todd?" Ed took a step back to let Todd study the engine. "I wouldn't mind a second opinion on this one."

The telephone rang. Ed wiped his hands on the grease rag hanging from his belt and reached to pick up the cordless phone on the bench nearby. "Mike's Garage, Ed speaking. May I help you?"

Lexi could hear someone talking quickly and loudly on the other end of the line.

"Sorry, Mike isn't here right now. He'll be back in a few minutes. Do you want to call then? No? A message, ah . . . well, all right." Ed put his hand over the mouthpiece. "Lexi, would you grab some paper and write this down?"

Lexi hurried into Mike's office and picked up a yellow pad and a pencil from the desk. She returned to Ed and handed him the notebook and pencil. "Here you go."

"No," Ed shook his head violently. "You write it down."

"But here's the paper and pencil . . ."

Ed took the phone from his ear and thrust it at Lexi. "You do it. Take the message."

"But wouldn't it be better if. . . ." Something in

Ed's look stopped Lexi cold. With a strange and sudden clarity, she realized that Ed was *not* going to take the message, no matter how many pencils she gave him. Lexi waved the phone away, saying, "You talk to the man. Tell me what he says. I'll write it down word for word."

Ed's features relaxed as he returned his attention to the receiver. "What was it you wanted to tell Mike? Start over again, please."

Before Lexi'd had time to repeat the message Ed had dictated to her, Mike returned.

"You just missed a phone call," Lexi told him. "Here's your message."

Mike read it and crumpled the paper in his hand. "Okay. Thanks. Appreciate it."

Lexi was tempted to comment to Todd on Ed's strange behavior concerning the message-taking incident, but before she had the opportunity, Mike distracted them all with an announcement.

"I bought Nancy roses. Do you think she'll like them?"

"Of course. What woman doesn't like roses?"

"But how many?" Mike challenged.

"A dozen," Todd guessed.

"Eighteen," Lexi interjected.

"Five hundred—or maybe a thousand," Ed speculated.

"What do you think I am? Made of money? I bought her five."

"Five roses? Why five? Why not half a dozen?"

"Five roses is just the right number for Nancy. I explained it to her in the card I sent with the flowers."

"Five roses," Lexi mused. "Now what does that mean?"

"Nancy deserves five roses because she's such a handful," Mike responded, a smug grin on his face.

Todd stared at the five fingers on his own hand. When he looked up, his eyes were twinkling. "Why, big brother, you're getting practically poetic in your old age."

"Great, isn't it? I didn't think I had it in me." Mike slapped Todd on the shoulder. "Let's see what you're doing inside this old jalopy. . . ."

All three men leaned beneath the hood of the car, and the odd phone incident between Ed and Lexi was forgotten.

———

"I'm amazed," Todd said bluntly as he and Lexi left the garage. "Ed has really whipped that place into shape. He's exactly what my brother needed. Ed's everything Mike used to be before he met Nancy."

"Don't be too hard on poor Nancy," Lexi said with a laugh. "She can't help it that she's so sweet and your brother's fallen head-over-heels in love with her."

"Well, when you put it that way . . ." Todd glanced at his wristwatch. "We still have some time. Let's stop at Egg and Binky's and see what's happening there. I'm curious to learn who won the argument over that contest Binky entered."

"No matter what happens, there isn't going to be a winner. Binky's homemaking skills are zilch, and Egg's aren't as good as hers. Whatever happens will be an unmitigated disaster."

"You don't have much faith in your friends," Todd teased. "Maybe Binky will whip together a twenty-five-layer cake that will astound the judges."

"Whatever those two do will amaze the judges, but I don't think it will earn many prizes."

It was a quick drive to their house. The Mc-Naughton home was large and slightly ramshackle. The yard appeared to need attention. The house was well-lived-in and well-loved, but not well-tended. All the first-floor windows were wide open. Todd and Lexi could hear bickering from the sidewalk.

"Turn on the fans," Binky's voice floated through the air.

"We don't have any fans!" Egg's panicked voice replied.

"There's one on the stove. Quick! Get that smell out of here."

"Do we have any air freshener? I can't quit coughing."

"Mom's going to kill us if she comes home and finds the house smelling like this!"

"What do you think is happening in there?" Todd whispered.

"Who knows?"

"Should we leave?"

"It might be safest," Lexi agreed, "but then we'll never know what's going on inside."

"I'm brave enough to knock if you're brave enough to enter." Todd squared his shoulders. "Nothing the McNaughtons have pulled has killed us yet."

"There's always a first time," Lexi said grimly as she pushed the doorbell.

The door flew open and slammed against the interior wall with a loud crack. Binky stood in the doorway. She was slapping a large dishtowel in the air and coughing. Smoke curled around the shape of her body.

"Is something on fire?" Lexi asked. "Have you called the fire department?"

"There's nothing on fire. Come inside. We're trying to get this smell out."

"Are you *sure* there's not a fire?" Todd looked around. "Usually when there's this much smoke, there's fire."

"It was just a little one in the bottom of the stove. Egg put it out. No problem."

Todd and Lexi walked reluctantly into the kitchen, where chaos reigned.

There were dirty dishes on every bit of counter space. Cereal, spoons, and bowls were stacked high. It appeared that every mixing bowl the McNaughtons had ever owned was displayed on the counter. The timers on both the oven and the microwave were buzzing in a raucous chorus.

The fan over the stove roared, sucking out the tendrils of smoke filling the air. The entire room smelled like a smokehouse. Lexi was reminded of dried beef, smoking hams, and burnt things in the bottom of a grill.

Egg stomped furiously through the kitchen waving a dishtowel and muttering something about burning down the entire house.

"Egg? Are you all right?" Todd asked.

Egg stopped flapping the towel long enough to glare at Todd. "Of course I'm not all right! My idiotic sister signed me up for some stupid contest so that she could go to the water park. I'm not 'all right' at all. I don't care if I ever go to this dumb water park.

What do I care if it means making a fool of myself in front of the entire school and burning my parents' home down in the process?"

"Oh, Egg. Just settle," Binky said cheerfully. "If you win the boom box, I'll let you keep it. It can be all yours. Won't that be nice?"

"There's not a boom box in the world worth this." Egg flung himself into a chair and leaned backward until only the two back legs of the chair were resting on the floor. "You'll never believe the wimpy, idiotic things Binky signed me up for."

"There's nothing wimpy or idiotic about any of it, Egg. They're good skills—things you need to know."

"When will I need to know how to sew a stuffed toy for an infant?" Egg demanded. "If I ever want to give a child a toy, I'll spare the poor kid and buy one at the store."

"I'll save the toy until you get married," Binky said primly. "And when you become a father and I become an aunt, I'll give it to your baby. You'll be so proud."

"You're sewing?" Todd gulped.

"A toy?" Lexi gasped.

"Why?" they asked in unison.

"Because Binky signed me up for the child-care competition. I either have to spend a week baby-sitting some little kid or make a toy that a child can play with. Have you ever heard of anything so stupid?" Egg held up the empty carcass of a teddy bear by one ear. It was flat, limp, and pitiful-looking. "This is how far I've gotten. Binky showed me how to use a sewing machine so I stitched up this . . . thing. I nearly sewed my finger to the fabric." Egg lifted his index finger to show Todd and Lexi the needle prick at its tip.

"Ow." Lexi winced. "I've gotten my fingertip caught in a sewing machine needle, Egg. That's painful."

"Now I'm supposed to *stuff* this stupid thing. Actually, where I'd like to stuff it is down my sister's throat." He glared at Binky. She smiled sweetly in return.

"She also signed me up for camping skills."

"That doesn't sound so bad, Egg. You like to camp."

"I think camping is great. Building bonfires and going fishing are fun. But do you know what I have to do for camping skills? Make beef jerky. Someone, somewhere, thinks that beef jerky prevents campers from starving." Egg waved his hand in the air at the dissipating cloud of smoke. "That's why it smells in here. I set my beef jerky on fire. The recipe said to cook it on low heat, but nothing seemed to be happening. I thought if I just turned the oven up a little bit . . ."

"All the way to 500 degrees," Binky interjected.

"I thought I'd be able to speed the process along." He nodded to a pile of charred rubble lying on a paper napkin next to the stove. "My beef jerky doesn't look so good, does it?"

"It looks like what's left over after a campfire," Lexi blurted. "Egg, if you don't remake that beef jerky, you won't win a trip to the water park."

"It'll be fine," Binky interjected cheerfully. "We're actually counting on Egg's peanut brittle to pull us out of this one."

"Egg's peanut brittle?" Todd choked. Lexi could tell he was having a difficult time subduing his laughter.

"Uh-huh. It's a microwave recipe."

"Egg, the microwave is beeping. You'd better take out your peanut brittle and pour it into a pan."

"Yeah, right." Egg picked up two pot holders and opened the microwave. Lexi could see a little puddle of caramel-colored goo sitting in a bowl.

Egg threw a few raw peanuts into the caramelized glob and poured it out across a piece of tinfoil in a pan.

"That's recognizable as peanut brittle," Lexi said hopefully. "It looks much better than the beef jerky."

"Do you think so?" Egg sounded hopeful for a moment. Then he dropped the bowl and began war dancing around the room, jumping on one foot and waving his hand in the air. "Ow! Ow! Ow! That stuff is hot. I burned my finger."

Binky opened the freezer door and pulled out a tray of ice. "Here, stick your hand in this. That'll cool it off. Quit being such a baby. You're not the only one with problems, you know."

"You mean you've got it worse than Egg?" Todd said with a chuckle. "I find that hard to believe."

"He's making a big deal out of this. He's really having a lot of fun. I can tell. I signed up for dressmaking, bread baking and candy making."

"Really, Binky? I didn't know you knew how to sew."

"Oh, I don't," Binky said calmly. "But I'm going to learn." She looked at her wristwatch. "I've got plenty of time."

"Binky, I'd bet money that you'll never wear anything that you sewed," Todd said, smirking.

"Good, then maybe I'll win two prizes. One from the school and one from you."

Egg held his finger on an ice cube in the tray. "When I tried to get out of this," he told Todd and Lexi, "I got a lecture from the home ec. teacher about how proud she was that I was participating in this very 'important event.' She told me how disappointed she'd be if I dropped out now. She said I was a 'role model' for my peers. A real nineties sort of guy. Do you believe it? Me? A nineties sort of guy?"

Lexi covered her mouth to keep from laughing.

"It's hard to imagine, isn't it? I always thought you were a cave man, Egg." Before her brother could respond, Binky patted him on the shoulders. "Everything's going to be fine. You've just hit a few bumpy patches, but they're no problem. Keep reminding yourself of the prizes we can win. You've got to have goals. Concentrate on the goals, not the little setbacks you have on the way."

Both Lexi and Todd had given up trying to control their laughter. Tears were streaming down Lexi's cheeks, and she could hardly catch her breath. Lexi clasped her hands to her stomach and rocked back and forth. "Oh, I'm laughing so hard my sides hurt."

"When is this contest?" Todd looked at the unstuffed teddy bear and the charred pile of beef jerky.

"We've still got a couple of days," Binky said calmly. "The contest's not until next week."

"How will you ever get all of it done in time?" Lexi asked. "You've never sewed before. Don't you think you might have a little trouble getting a dress made in just a few days?"

"It never hurts a person to go without sleep for a few hours," Binky said nonchalantly. "Besides, I've already got the pattern laid out. See?" She pointed to the table in the dining room. Fabric and pattern pieces were scattered helter-skelter across the table.

Lexi winced, knowing that if Binky were ever going to make heads or tails of that dress, she would have to start by sorting out the mess. "Do you want some help? I'd be happy to work with you."

"Oh, I'm sure I won't need it," Binky said, oozing with confidence, "but thanks anyway."

Egg sat hunched in his chair, glaring at his sister.

"It's too bad you guys are so busy," Todd commented. "You're going to miss the party."

"What party?" Egg perked up.

"Mike's girlfriend Nancy told me to invite you to her place for a barbecue tomorrow."

"Us too?" Binky looked puzzled. "Why?"

"Nancy said she'd never met anyone named Egg, and she thought she'd like to. Besides, she's heard so much about my friends that she wants to meet all of you. You can come too, of course, Lexi."

"That's very sweet," Lexi said. "I'd love to go to Nancy's."

"Me too," Binky chimed.

"What about your dress, Binky? And your bread baking and candy making?"

"I'll get it all done. No problem. I'll stay up all night to sew this dress. If it takes me until morning, that's the way it'll be."

"What about you, Egg?"

Egg held up the teddy bear. It swung pitifully from the end of his hand. "I'm going to stuff this rotten little bear tonight, and then I'm done."

"You can't turn in beef jerky that looks like that, can you?" Lexi asked.

"Watch me. There's no way I'm missing out on food and fun to stuff a bear or be a jerk making jerky."

Egg's expression turned wistful. "I wish the barbecue would last through the entire weekend so I wouldn't have to be in this dumb contest at all."

"Oh, Egg, don't be so glum. We have time tonight to work on our projects. We'll be ready to go to Nancy's tomorrow."

"Okay," Todd said doubtfully. "We'll pick you up at four." He backed slowly toward the door. "We'd better not stay any longer. You two have a lot to accomplish between now and tomorrow. Good luck."

Todd and Lexi escaped quickly. It wasn't until they reached Todd's car that they burst into gales of laughter.

"Did you see that kitchen? I thought World War III had struck in there!"

"Egg's beef jerky looked like a pile of burnt toast."

"And that poor little bear! He'll scare any child Egg tries to give it to." Lexi leaned back against the seat of the car and laughed until tears streamed down her cheeks.

"Every time I think it's impossible for Egg and Binky to do something more far-out and wacky than they've already done, they come up with something new that exceeds my wildest expectations."

"Egg's not going to win any prizes," Todd said. "If Binky wants that trip to the water park, I think she's on her own."

"I don't want to downplay Binky's abilities, but it's pretty difficult to learn how to sew a dress in one evening."

"Binky's a determined girl; she'll figure it out," Todd assured her.

"Do you think Egg will get his projects done?"

"Sure," Todd frowned. "Frankly, it's Binky that I'm worried about."

"Why? I thought you said she'd be okay."

"Because I think there's a good chance that Egg might strangle her before she gets her dress finished."

Chapter Seven

"Here it is," Todd announced as they pulled up at the front door of Nancy's house on Saturday afternoon. The flower beds in the yard were a mass of color, and the neatly painted bungalow was warm and inviting.

Nancy stood in the doorway wearing a big white apron and a chef's hat tilted jauntily to one side. She waved a spatula. "Come inside," she yelled. "We just put the burgers on the grill."

Todd and Lexi, Binky and Egg followed Nancy into the house. The interior of the house spoke even more eloquently of Nancy's personality. Cross-country skis and tennis rackets filled the corners of the foyer, and a basketball sat in a place of honor on a rocking chair in the living room.

"Sorry about all the sports equipment," Nancy apologized, "but when I'm not at the hospital, I like to work out. It takes away some of that excess energy and tension I develop at work."

There were family pictures and photos of Mike scattered all over the room.

"You've got a big family," Lexi commented.

"Three brothers and three sisters," Nancy replied. "I wanted to be the fourth son in the family.

My big brothers taught me to lift weights, snare go-phers, and play baseball." As Nancy spoke about her childhood, Lexi saw a glimmer of pain in her new friend's expression.

On the way to the kitchen, they passed the dining room. One entire wall in Nancy's dining room was covered with whimsical paintings of clowns. Nancy followed Lexi's gaze.

"What can I say? I like sports, kids, flowers, and clowns," Nancy commented.

The kitchen was full of delicious aromas. Nancy handed Egg a bowl of potato salad, and Binky picked up a tray of buns.

"Todd, grab some hot pads from the drawer and take the baked beans out of the oven. Lexi, would you get that big bowl of fruit from the refrigerator?"

Nancy was brisk and efficient. "Ed and Mike are already out back. You came just in time. Ed was dy-ing to put the burgers on the grill, so I told him to go ahead."

They stepped out the back door and onto a large redwood deck, where Ed hovered over the grill. He wore an apron that proclaimed in bold letters "Kiss the Cook" and a chef's hat with "Cook" emblazoned across it.

Mike was sprawled in a hammock holding a glass of iced tea and giving Ed cooking instructions.

Lexi laughed. "Hey, Ed, with an apron like that, you'd better watch out."

"What . . . huh?" Ed stammered, looking up from the grill. A frown creased his forehead, then he looked down at his apron. "Oh, yeah." He grinned uneasily then hurried on, "So, how do you guys like your burgers? Well done? Rare? Medium? Speak now or forever hold your peace." He twirled the spatula in his hand.

"No matter what you tell him, all the burgers are going to turn out the same anyway," Mike commented. "But you might as well make him happy and put in your order."

"Don't listen to him," Ed said. "I happen to be the world's finest hamburger flipper. In fact, if there were a hamburger-flipping olympics, I would win the gold medal."

"Then you'd better start flipping. I think that burger in the middle is starting to burn."

Egg and Binky placed their dishes of food on the picnic table and sat down. Neither one spoke. Mike rolled out of the hammock and stood up.

"What's wrong with you guys?" he asked. "You look terrible."

"Thanks. That makes me feel a lot better," Binky said with a hint of sarcasm.

Egg turned to Mike. "We were up all night."

"Problems?" Mike was immediately concerned. "Trouble at home?"

"Yeah, *lots* of trouble. Binky signed us up for this stupid contest at the school. She wants to win a trip to the water park or a boom box, but at the rate we're going, we're going to be laughed out of the contest."

"What kind of contest?" Mike came to the picnic table and sat down across from them. "Tell me more about it."

Binky explained how she'd wanted to visit the new water park and had finally found her opportunity. "I thought if both Egg and I entered we'd have a doubly good chance of winning. Don't you think that was a good idea, Mike?"

"Sounds sensible to me. What is it you're supposed to make for this contest?"

"Egg is in the child-care division," Binky explained. "He either had to take care of a child or sew a toy for a child, and he decided that it would be easier to sew a toy."

"Except I don't know anything about sewing," Egg confessed. "Actually, though, the sewing wasn't so bad, but last night I tried to stuff it. No matter what I do, that dumb teddy bear looks like the Hunchback of Notre Dame."

"That's one deformed bear." Mike tried to hide a smile. "Maybe you could pretend you did it on purpose?"

Egg's eyes lit. "That's an idea. It actually doesn't look much like a teddy bear anyway. Maybe I could tell the judges it's a stuffed baboon."

"Or a camel. It looks a little bit like a camel," Binky offered. "With those humps in the back and all."

"I don't know, either one might work. Which do you think a little kid would like more, a stuffed baboon or a stuffed camel?"

Mike rolled his eyes, but he didn't laugh. "Binky, what have you been doing for the contest?"

"I spent last night baking buns."

"She's lying. She didn't bake buns," Egg said flatly.

"Did too."

"Did not."

"Did too."

"Binky, admit it. What you baked were hockey pucks."

"Maybe they *looked* like hockey pucks, and

maybe they *tasted* like hockey pucks, but they're supposed to be buns."

"Too bad there isn't a sports category in this contest," Egg said. "Because you have the best hockey pucks I've ever seen."

Fortunately, at that moment, Ed called out, "Hamburgers are ready."

"Great! Let's eat." Nancy clapped her hands.

"Is there anything you want me to do, honey?" Mike asked. He moved toward Nancy and put an arm around her waist.

"Will you come inside with me and help me carry out the lemonade and the glasses?"

When they'd disappeared into the kitchen, Binky giggled.

"What's so funny?"

"Mike and Nancy are acting like old married people already, don't you think?" A grin of pleasure broke across her face. "I think it's so romantic."

"Binky, you think everything is romantic," Egg accused.

"Not everything." Binky giggled again. "I don't think your teddy bear is romantic. I think that looks like something out of a bad dream."

"Here we are, ready to eat. World's best hamburgers from the world's best hamburger chef." Ed set a plate of burgers on the table. "Ketchup, mustard, salt, pepper, onions, pickles? Everything you could possibly want for a deluxe burger. Where are our host and hostess?" Nancy and Mike had not returned from the kitchen. Ed put his hands over his eyes. "Probably smooching over the lemonade, right?"

"It wouldn't surprise me a bit," Todd muttered.

Just then Nancy and Mike burst through the back door. Nancy's cheeks were flushed and she wore a smile.

"I was right." Ed and Todd exchanged a knowing glance.

Binky sighed and muttered under her breath, "So romantic . . ."

"Mike, do you want to say grace?" Nancy asked when they were all seated around the table.

Mike nodded willingly. "Dear Lord," he began, "thank you for this food and these friends. Thanks especially, Lord, for sending Ed to us to help us organize our lives. Take care of Egg and Binky through this contest. Help them to know that someday they're going to look back on this time with fond memories. And thanks especially, Lord, for Nancy, who's brightened my life so much. Amen."

"Let's eat." Egg lunged for the fluffy buns piled high on the plate. "Look, Binky, these are what buns are supposed to look like."

"That's okay, Egg, just because your teddy bear looks like a baboon, and my buns look like hockey pucks, doesn't mean we can't win the contest yet. We still have a few hours to get things done."

"Binky's trying to get me to redo my beef jerky," Egg explained to Todd.

"You mean that stuff you nearly set the house on fire with?"

"We got most of the smell out of the house before my folks came home. We just told them that I'd used a little too much liquid smoke in my recipe."

"Mike, we might have to visit that contest at the school next week," Nancy commented.

"It might be entertaining."

"Did you work today, Nancy?" Lexi inquired.

"I work tomorrow. The early shift. I'm eager to get back to the hospital. There was a preemie born when I was on duty the other night, and I want to see how he's doing. He was so tiny and sweet. The doctor was worried about his lungs. I want to see how everything turned out."

"It must be hard to be a nurse," Binky commented.

"In some ways it is, but in other ways, it's the most wonderful career. There are so many opportunities to help people, to make them feel more comfortable or better about themselves. Working with the babies is great because you see them grow and blossom. Then you can send them home with their parents. I love what I do. It's very rewarding."

"What about the sick babies. The babies that don't live?" Lexi asked softly.

"It's very difficult. That doesn't happen often, but when it does, it breaks my heart. You'd better be careful not to get me started talking about my babies, Lexi," Nancy warned. "I'm very possessive. When a baby is born on my shift, I consider him or her 'mine' until they go home. I'm like an old mother grizzly bear protecting my young."

"Sometimes when I go to the hospital," Mike said, "to pick Nancy up, I'll find her in the nursery, still rocking a baby even after her shift is past."

"They can't get too much loving, you know." Nancy caught sight of Egg's empty plate. "Egg, don't quit eating. Look at all the food we have! Todd warned me about your appetite. I made double everything. You're not going to disappoint me, are you?"

Egg brightened. "Well, if you're *expecting* me to eat . . ."

Later, while Nancy, Lexi, and Mike were doing dishes, Ed and Todd set up the volleyball net. When it became too chilly for volleyball, they all moved inside to Nancy's living room.

"Now what?" Mike asked. "You're the one who likes to play games, Nancy. Have you got any suggestions?"

"How about charades? Everyone loves charades, don't they?"

Lexi noticed the odd expression on Ed's face. "Ed? You want to play, don't you?" she asked softly.

"Huh? Oh, yeah, sure. I guess so. I'm not very good at it though."

They divided into teams. Lexi, Ed, and Egg took on Nancy, Mike, Todd, and Binky.

"Here's your clue." Nancy handed a slip of paper to Ed. "Read this, and then act it out for your teammates. If they can get it, you get a point. If they don't get it, we get the point."

"Don't bother with the paper," Ed said as he brushed Nancy's hand away. "Just whisper the clue in my ear."

"Okay, if that's the way you want to do it," Nancy said. Ed leaned close to her in order to hear what she was saying.

It became apparent to Lexi after several rounds that Ed always refused to read the clue when it was his turn to do a charade. Instead, he would have someone from the other team whisper it into his ear. However, it didn't matter how Ed chose to play the game, because Lexi's team won by four points.

"You really hammered us," Mike complained.

"There must be another game we could win at."

"I know one! Our family used to do this when we were kids." Nancy picked up a newspaper. "All you have to do is pick out a headline from a page of the paper. Then your team writes three other headlines just as believable as the real one. Read the four headlines aloud, and the other team has to pick out the real headline from the phony ones. If you can do it, you get a point. The team with the most points wins."

"That sounds fun."

"Let's try it."

Suddenly, amid the enthusiasm, Ed jumped to his feet. "Excuse me," he said. "I've got to use the bathroom." He was gone a long time, and when he returned he was very pale.

"Are you all right?" Mike asked.

"I'm just a little tired," Ed admitted. "I was up at five A.M. this morning." He looked at his watch. "If you don't mind, I'll just pass on this game and go home."

"We don't mind. I hope you're feeling okay."

"I am. No problem," Ed assured them. "I just need a little rest."

That's odd, Lexi thought. Ed had been fine until Nancy had suggested playing the newspaper game. But why would a game make Ed so upset he'd want to leave? It didn't make sense.

Even so, Lexi was beginning to feel more and more strongly that there was something mysterious about Ed Bell.

Chapter Eight

"Are you sure you don't want a ride home?" Todd offered. "It'll only take me a couple of minutes to run you back to your place."

"Nah, it's all right," Egg said. "Binky and I need the exercise. Besides, you aren't ready to leave yet. We'd stay too if we didn't have to get ready for this stupid competition."

"It's not a stupid competition, Egg."

"Is too."

"Is not."

"Is too."

Binky and Egg disappeared down the sidewalk.

Todd returned to the living room laughing and shaking his head.

"Those two are something else," Mike commented as Todd sat down in the recliner.

"I've never met anyone else quite like them," Nancy agreed. "They're . . . unique . . . but I like them. I can tell, in spite of all the bickering, that they really love life—and each other."

Lexi curled contentedly into a corner of the couch and buried her toes in a throw pillow. "This has been a great night. Good food, good company, lots of fun. Thanks, Nancy." Unconsciously, Lexi unfolded her arms and rubbed her hands against her upper arms. "Are you chilly?"

"Just a little. I was fine until I sat down."

Nancy jumped up from her spot on the love seat next to Mike. "Why don't I get you a sweater? You'll feel better."

Lexi took the sweater that Nancy offered and draped it over her shoulders. "Ah, much better." She snuggled back into her corner of the couch.

Todd picked up the photo album lying on Nancy's coffee table and began to look at it. He studied the first picture. "Who's this?"

"That's me. Can't you tell?"

"You looked entirely different back then. I suppose it's your hair." Todd stood up and moved to the couch where Lexi sat. "Look at this."

Lexi peered at the picture. Staring back at her was an attractive, long-haired girl with a lot of dark eye makeup and a somber expression on her face. In her hand, the girl held a half-smoked cigarette.

It was a dramatic change from the person Lexi saw tonight. In the photo, Nancy looked tough and old, as if she were coated with a hard, unpleasant veneer. None of the photos had captured Nancy smiling. In almost every picture, a cigarette dangled either from her fingertips or from the corner of her lips.

"I can hardly believe this is you," Todd commented. "You seem so different now. So much . . . softer . . . and prettier." Todd blushed until he was pink from the base of his neck to the roots of his hair. "That didn't come out quite right. I'm sorry, Nancy. You were pretty then and you're pretty now."

"It's okay. You didn't say anything to make me uncomfortable or hurt my feelings. In fact, I think you're sweet.

"I *am* different now, Todd. I'm a 'new' person. Have you read that verse in 2 Corinthians 5:17? 'If anyone belongs to Christ, then he is made new. The old things have gone; everything is made new!' That's me. I've been made new," Nancy said with a wide smile. "And I'm proud of it. There isn't much to be proud about where the old me is concerned."

"I don't believe that," Todd protested.

"Do believe it, Todd. The girl in those pictures was not a happy person. She wasn't even a very nice person."

"You? Not nice?" Lexi couldn't believe it as she stared at Nancy, glowing and content, tucked into the curve of Mike's arm.

Nancy looked at Mike and said softly, "I think it's time I told them about the old me."

Mike nodded.

"Though I seem perfectly mainstream and run-of-the-mill now," Nancy began, "I was a very rebellious, unhappy teenager."

Lexi thought of her friends who'd been like that in the past. Jennifer Golden had become difficult until it was discovered that she had a learning disorder. Matt Windsor had had a rocky time when his home life was disrupted. Had Nancy had something similar go wrong in her life?

"I did a lot of things I've since regretted," Nancy continued. "I skipped school so often that I was nearly held back. It's a good thing that didn't happen, or I might never have graduated from high school.

"I spent a lot of time with my friends haunting the malls, shoplifting whatever I could. I even had a 'fence' who'd take the things I stole and sell them again. That's how I earned the money I used to buy alcohol, cigarettes, and occasional drugs."

A regretful expression flickered across Nancy's features. "I thought my parents were dumb as stones back then. I was positive they'd never had a life of their own. If they'd had one, it was surely so dull and uninteresting that it wasn't worth knowing about. I thought my parents were small-minded, provincial, and boring. What's more, they had problems of their own.

"Just to spite them, I picked friends that I knew they'd hate. I hung out with a crowd that frightened them. Looking back, I realize that the people I was drawn to were wild and bad. My group had no value system. My friends during that time had loose morals and little conscience. Now I see how dangerous that type of person can be. At the time, however, I believed they were exciting. They made me feel like I was part of the 'in' crowd. Since my biggest fear was being 'out,' they filled my needs perfectly."

"This doesn't sound like you at all, Nancy," Lexi murmured.

"Oh, it's not the person I am now. It's the person I was back then." Nancy looked lovingly at Mike. "If I were the same now as I was back then, I would never have met Mike or fallen in love."

"What made you change?" Todd was obviously trying to comprehend all that was being said.

"I was on a downhill slide that finally hit bottom," Nancy said bluntly. "One night I was part of a group that stole a car."

"Nancy!" Lexi gasped. "I can't believe it."

"Me either," Todd chimed.

"It was hard for me to accept at first too," Mike admitted. He squeezed Nancy's hand. "But like

Nancy said, she's a new person now."

"I spent the night in jail, and my father bailed me out in the morning. It should have been embarrassing and humiliating. Instead, it just hardened my resolve to rebel against the system." Nancy shook her head. "My poor parents. The sleep they must have lost and the worry they must have had because of me! It's a wonder they're still speaking to me."

"Maybe you don't want to tell us all these things. . . ."

"Oh, but I do." Nancy smiled at Todd. "I talk about my past as often as I can, especially to teenagers. It's always my hope that they will learn something from my mistakes."

"What happened after the stolen car?" Lexi asked.

"My parents really lowered the boom. They put bars on my windows and locks on my door and forced me to stay in at night. Somehow, with all their strict monitoring, I managed to graduate from high school." Nancy gave a wry laugh. "I thought that I was going to be free then, leave home and get away from all the rules and regulations."

"Did you?"

"It turned out that my parents had more self-discipline and determination than even I did." Her voice still held awe as she spoke of it. "They actually forced me to go to college. They told me they would pay for my education, room and board and would continue to do so if I got passing grades. If I decided to return to the streets to be with my friends, they told me that I'd be cut off from them forever. Even as hardened as I was at that time, I knew that I didn't want to lose my parents completely. Therefore, unwillingly, I went to college."

"What happened?"

"Even though I didn't want to admit it to my family, I liked school. I was excited by the classes and the learning. I enjoyed the teachers and the friends I made there. My friends in college were different than those I'd known in high school. Unfortunately, my old friends still had some sort of evil grip on my mind. After a year, I dropped out of college just to prove that my parents couldn't force me to do anything that I didn't want to do."

"But the person you were hurting most was yourself!" Lexi exclaimed.

"I know. Stupid, wasn't it? I still had a chip on my shoulder and felt like I had something to prove to my parents. All the frustration and hostility I'd been hoarding for that year at college came out once I dropped out."

"I don't understand. What do you mean?" Lexi asked.

"In some sick, perverted sense, I felt like punishing my parents for loving me and trying to restrict me. So, as soon as college was out in the spring, I moved in with a man I'd met in a bar."

"But you weren't old enough to be in a bar."

"I had a fake ID. You have no idea how wretched I was during that time, Lexi. I'm almost ashamed to talk about it."

"You don't have to, you know," Todd assured her.

"It's okay. This is something you need to know, Todd. I'm in love with your brother, and it wouldn't be fair to keep secrets from Mike's family. Anyway, the fellow with whom I moved in was complete scum. Slime from the bottom of the water barrel. Sludge from *underneath* the water barrel. I don't believe there was anyone lower or sleazier or creepier than that guy. He didn't want to work, but he didn't mind letting me work. So for a year, I waited tables in a cafe earning enough to pay the rent and put food on the table."

"What a sleazeball!" Todd exclaimed.

"He was that and worse. During the time I lived with him, he was heavily into drugs and was sleeping with other women. And do you know what the really sick part about all this was? *I didn't care.* I had no self-esteem or self-worth left. I thought that I deserved a man this bad, this crude, this careless. And without any self-esteem, I seemed to have no brakes. There were no barriers I didn't want to break. No little voice in my head telling me to stop when things got out of hand. It was as though my conscience was numbed. If it *did* talk to me, I refused to listen."

Nancy folded her hands in her lap and stared at the floor. When she began to speak again, her voice was soft and wistful. "I did a lot of things I'm ashamed of now. I let that man abuse me in so many ways, but when I left him, I was just as promiscuous and despicable as he had been. I left him in my apartment and moved in with another man. For an entire year, I wandered around lost, confused, and bent on destroying myself."

Lexi and Todd sat together on the couch, their hands entwined, staring at Nancy and Mike.

Lexi didn't understand. None of what Nancy was telling them made sense. Beautiful, healthy, cheerful Nancy? How could she be this vile person she kept insisting she once was? And Mike! How could he just sit there with his arm around her and not even flinch at the dreadful story Nancy was telling?

Then Mike squeezed Nancy's hand and leaned forward. He looked intently from his brother to Lexi. "I'm sure you're wondering how I can calmly listen to this, but Nancy told me everything about her past soon after we met. There are no secrets between us.

"Although Nancy's made some disastrous decisions, I'm not perfect myself. It might have been easy to condemn or criticize her for the way she'd lived her life and to walk away, but I began to think about how God views sin," Mike continued softly. "Because He is perfect, in His sight, *all* sin is evil. Therefore, could I *really* say that Nancy's sins were 'big' ones and mine were 'small'? I didn't think so.

"We're *both* sinners. The Bible says that everyone has fallen away from God. Not one of us is able to get back to Him by our own devices. Once I realized that, it was easy for me to forgive Nancy. After all, God had forgiven her already.

"It was her honesty about her life that impressed me most. I'd never met a person who'd been through so many bad situations and made something good come from them. I wanted to know her better. I *needed* to know her better. I hadn't planned on falling in love," Mike admitted. "Being in love seemed to be more trouble than it was worth. Until I met Nancy, that is."

"Tell us how you changed, Nancy."

"I woke up one morning and realized that I didn't know where I was or with whom I was sleeping. I didn't know where I'd been or what I'd done the night before. I looked at the man in the bed next to me and was stunned by how low I'd sunk and how little respect I'd had for myself. I literally crawled out of that apartment and took stock of my life. For the first time it seemed clear to me what a self-destructive path I'd been on and how blind and deaf I'd been to my family."

Nancy shuddered. "It was the most frightening time in my entire life. I'd burned all my bridges. I'd been cruel and callous to my parents. I'd laughed at their values and their beliefs. I'd told them I didn't need them, but there I was, needing them more than I ever had before in my life. I had to consider crawling back to people I hadn't spoken to in over a year."

"What did you do?" Lexi asked softly. "What happened?"

"I went home," Nancy said simply. "I walked out of the life I'd been living with only the clothes on my back, and I went home."

"And . . ."

"And my parents were waiting for me. They welcomed me with open arms and open hearts. My room was just as I'd left it. Only the sheets on the bed had been changed. My mother cried and told me I was too thin. She started to cook my favorite foods. My father cried and told me I was beautiful. I must have looked like a real wreck by the time I got home. My clothes were filthy. Dad took me to my room and opened the closet door. My clothes were still hanging there, just as I'd left them." Nancy smiled ruefully, "The teddy bear I'd had since I was a child was even perched on my bed.

"Todd, do you and Lexi remember the story of the prodigal son in the Bible? That's how I felt. Like a child who'd run away and was afraid to come home— terrified of how his family might greet him. Then, when I arrived, I discovered they'd been waiting for me all along. My parents didn't greet me with criticism or scorn. They took me to their hearts with love, affection, and acceptance. They did it, just like in the Bible."

"Then what? Could you pick up where you'd left off?"

"No. I hadn't 'left off' at a very pretty spot in my life. I told you how rebellious I'd been. I didn't want to be that kind of person anymore. I was so moved by the way my parents had welcomed me home with their love and forgiveness that I thought I'd give the God they kept talking about a try. For years I'd tuned them out whenever they talked about their faith. I'd refused to go to church with them on Sundays. I'd laughed in their faces, and I'd laughed behind their backs about the silly fantasy they had about a Savior. But, the way *I'd* chosen to live my life didn't work out, so I decided to give *theirs* a try.

"I certainly couldn't do any worse for myself. My parents told me that the way they'd survived my absence was by turning to God. I decided that if He'd helped them to stay strong while I was falling apart, maybe He could help me pull myself back together. There was one hitch, of course."

"What was that?"

"There was no way I could believe that God would accept anyone like me. If this God was perfect, why would He want to have anything to do with me? It was almost unthinkable to me that my parents had been able to forgive and accept me. I didn't even know this God of theirs. Why should He want to do anything for me?"

Nancy's smile was sweet and thoughtful. "I had a lot of lessons to learn, didn't I? The biggest one was about forgiveness. I saw it all around me. I received it from my parents. I felt it from God. Yet it was very difficult for me to forgive *myself* for what I'd done. It wasn't until I finally came to grips with the fact that God had forgiven me for things I couldn't forgive myself for that I could let go. I finally learned to start looking forward and to quit looking back. Psalm 103:12 says, 'He has taken our sins away from us as far as the east is from west.' Amazing, huh?"

Mike picked up Nancy's hand and traced the outline of her palm with his finger. "Now we're coming to the part that I like best."

"What *did* happen next, Nancy?"

"After a few weeks of good food and unqualified love and affection, I began to feel strong and whole again. I knew that I had to do everything in my power to resist the pull back to my old lifestyle. I thought the best way to do that would be to go back to school. My dad nearly jumped for joy the first time I mentioned college. He hopped into the car and drove me to the university to pick up catalogs and talk to the dean. As it turned out, they were only one week into the semester. In only a few minutes, I was a college student again!

"That first semester I had to take whatever classes were still open to me. Ironically, they turned out to be classes I loved and wanted to pursue. I discovered that I had a real facility for the sciences. Biology, anatomy, chemistry. I loved them all.

"And the other thing I realized I loved? Children. They were so pure and so innocent, untarnished by all the things that had happened to me in my life. I had this overwhelming urge to protect them in some way. I'd messed up my life, but I didn't want to see any more children mess up theirs.

"I struggled as to how I could blend my two loves, science and children. For a while I considered being a teacher. But after an education class or two, I realized that wasn't what I wanted at all. I did know, however, what I was supposed to be."

"A pediatric nurse," Todd finished triumphantly.

"Exactly." A pleased grin spread across Nancy's features. "It was the most perfect job I could think of. Working with little ones every day, making sure they got a healthy start in life. Loving them when they had to be away from their mothers.

"Once I decided to be a pediatric nurse, I was obsessed by it. I couldn't finish with school nearly soon enough to satisfy myself. The crazy part about it was when I was just drifting along, I'd earned D's and F's in school. And now, when I was pushing myself so hard that some days I thought I might drop, I couldn't keep myself off the honor roll. I even managed a couple of A pluses. Can you believe it? Me? Miss I-Hate-School and I-Hate-Life?"

"What a turnaround," Lexi murmured.

"I was given a gift, Lexi, a second chance at life. I wasn't going to waste this one like I had the first go-around. I graduated from college *summa cum laude*, got a job at the hospital and," Nancy spread her hands wide in an expansive gesture, "this is where I am today."

"It's hard for me to believe those things you told us about yourself, Nancy. About the drugs and the men." Todd glanced at his brother. "And I'm really surprised that Mike never mentioned any of this before. Didn't it bother you?"

"It did at first," Mike admitted, "but Nancy told

me about her past early in our relationship. I had fair warning before I fell in love. She didn't want me to become involved with her if I couldn't handle her past. But I understand why it was so easy for her parents to accept her back into their lives. There's no one more loving, giving, or caring than Nancy. Her parents have forgiven her. God has forgiven her. There's no reason for *me* to hold a grudge. There are no secrets between us. She loves me and I love her. Here and now—in the present and for the future. The past is past. Dead, gone, buried."

"As far as east is from west," Lexi murmured.

"Exactly. Farther than we can even fathom."

"It seems so awful to think of you . . . that way," Lexi said softly.

"The men, the drugs, the wild living, you mean?" Nancy asked bluntly.

"Yes. I know I live a sheltered life. My parents have always protected me. It seems like such a hard and painful life."

"It is. I was being used, Lexi. Used by men. Used by people I thought were my friends."

"Then you have regrets?"

"Lots of them. I particularly regret my promiscuous lifestyle." Nancy was brutally honest. "Now that I've found a man who loves me as much as Mike does, a man I love with all my heart, I'd like to wipe all those mistakes away, but I can't. I'd like to be 'brand-new' for Mike. Every time those regrets become too overwhelming, I just have to remind myself that I've been forgiven. God made me brand-new. What's most wonderful of all is that Mike loves and accepts me, past and all. The fact that he can know my past and still love me boggles my mind." Nancy's impish grin returned. "I'll have to keep reminding him of my best traits and try to divert him from my worst."

She took Mike's hand between her palms and held it to her cheek. "I believe that Mike is another gift from God. I'm going to treasure him forever."

"Isn't this where the violin starts playing and little fat cupids fly through the air shooting love arrows into you?" Todd grinned.

"Todd," Lexi poked him in the ribs, "don't tease your brother."

"Look at those two." Todd inclined his head toward Mike and Nancy as they stared, smitten, into each other's eyes. "They don't even know we're here. All they can see is each other."

Nancy winked at Todd. "Just because I've got my eyes on your brother doesn't mean I can't hear what you're saying." She gave Mike a quick peck on the cheek and turned back to Todd and Lexi. "All I can say is that I've never been happier. I feel, finally, that my life is beginning. And," she said, with a stern look settling across her features, "I hope that you two have been listening carefully to what I had to say. I don't want anyone else to learn the lessons I've learned the hard way. Living according to God's rules is the right way, not the sissy way. Don't ever forget that."

Todd and Lexi were subdued and silent after they left Nancy's house. Neither spoke until Todd pulled into the driveway of the Leighton home.

"Todd? Are you going to be all right?" Lexi asked.

"Me? Why?"

"You learned a lot of things about your brother's girlfriend tonight. Some of them might have been pretty hard to take."

Todd looked thoughtfully across the steering wheel and down the driveway, his eyes fixed on some distant point that Lexi could not see. "I thought I'd be more upset than I am," he said frankly. "But I admire Nancy's honesty. I respect her more now than I ever have before."

Lexi nodded, understanding. "I feel the same way. She's been very brave. With God's help she turned her life around. I think the announcement is going to come pretty soon, Todd. You're going to have a sister-in-law."

Todd grinned into the darkness. "She's going to be a great one."

Chapter Nine

"Hey, wait up," Binky yelled as Lexi turned a corner in the school hallway. She trotted toward Lexi, huffing and puffing, her face pink. Binky's hair was pulled back in an unflattering ponytail, and her bangs stuck up in clumps as though she'd been tugging on them.

"What's wrong with you? You look as though you didn't go to bed last night," Lexi observed.

"I didn't," Binky said. "I'm doing everything in my power to stay awake. If I weren't working so hard at keeping my eyes open, I'd bet money that there isn't a teacher in this school who could keep me awake. Do you realize how boring everyone is?"

"Everyone but you, Bink," Lexi said with a laugh.

Binky grabbed Lexi by the arm. "Lexi, you've got to help me. I can't do it alone. You're the only one who can save me. You've got to help me. Please say yes. Please. Please, please, please."

"What are you talking about?" Lexi tried to uncurl Binky's clenched fingers from her blouse. "Has something terrible happened?"

"*You* might not think it's terrible, but *I* do. I need help. I can't sew that dress for the contest by myself. You've got to help me."

"The dress?" Lexi burst out laughing. "Is that all?"

"Is that all?" Binky squealed. "Isn't that enough? I stayed up all night cutting the stupid thing out."

"That shouldn't have taken long," Lexi commented.

"Huh! Tell me about it. The fabric is a jungle print in black and white. There are faces of lions and tigers all over it. Some of the faces go this way, some of them go that way, and a few of them go that direction." Binky pointed up, down, and sideways. "I didn't want the animals' faces to be upside down, but there's no way I could figure out to make them all right side up. Finally, I decided I'd have to do it any way I could. The fabric was swimming before my eyes, so I just started cutting. Now I'm afraid that the animals might be running *sideways* across the dress. I don't think the home ec. teacher will approve of that. I seem to remember something about the fabric needing to head in the same direction."

"I'm sure it will be fine, Binky." Lexi tried not to giggle. "I'll be glad to take a look at your dress after school."

"What if I've ruined it already? Everybody's going to notice. They'll all laugh and say, 'What is that stupid Binky McNaughton doing here anyway? She's no homemaker, she's an idiot!' "

Tears pooled in the corners of Binky's eyes. "Oh, Lexi, I'm so sorry I entered this contest."

"Binky, I'll help you with the dress. Don't worry about it."

"It's not just the dress," Binky wailed. "Egg decided to make another batch of beef jerky last night after we got home from Nancy's."

"Did he burn it?"

"No, but it's so stringy and tough that dentists could use it to pull teeth. And that's not the worst of it."

"There's more?"

"Dad decided he wanted to taste Egg's peanut brittle, and he loosened a crown on his tooth. Now *he* has to go to the dentist. He told Egg never to make peanut brittle again." Binky groaned and put the heels of her hands to her forehead. "Why do I always act before I think, Lexi? Egg and I are the most klutzy people I've ever met. What made me think that we could cook and sew?"

"You're an eternal optimist, Binky. There's nothing wrong with that. You wanted a trip to the water park or a boom box and saw a potential way to get there, that's all. I admire you for that."

"You wouldn't if you broke your teeth on Egg's peanut brittle or saw my sideways dress," Binky said glumly.

"Just relax, I'll be over after school to help you with the dress. I've done a lot of sewing, and I'm sure that you haven't done anything that we can't fix." Lexi smiled cheerfully at her friend, even though deep down inside she wasn't convinced that the dress could be saved.

"I really appreciate this. Thank you, thank you, thank you. You are truly my dearest friend in the entire world."

Some of the animation and light came back into Binky's eyes. She straightened and brushed her bangs into a more presentable appearance. "I feel much better, thanks to you. I'll bet there's still a chance that Egg and I can win that trip to the water

park. After all, who else has a practically profes-
sional seamstress like you to help them? Oh, Lexi,
this is going to be great. I can hardly wait."

"I'm glad I made you feel better," Lexi said with
a laugh. "Don't be worried if I don't get to your place
right after school. I borrowed a sweater from Nancy
last night and forgot to give it back to her. I'm going
to drop it off at the garage so Mike can take it to her
this evening. Then I'll come to your house and see
what we can do to rescue your dress."

What Lexi didn't add was that it was Binky who
actually needed rescuing . . . from herself.

After school, Lexi walked down the sidewalk
humming to herself. As she neared Mike's garage,
she noticed that the street was very quiet. No more
cars were parked in line waiting to be serviced. Since
Ed's appearance, things had become much more or-
ganized around the shop.

"Hello? Anybody here?" Lexi called from the
doorway. There was no response. Lexi stepped into
the garage and called again. "Mike? Ed? Are you
here?" Still silence.

Lexi walked through the garage, peering behind
vehicles. There was no sign of life. Finally, she went
to the door of Mike's office. Tapping lightly on the
door with one hand, she turned the knob with the
other and poked her head inside.

"Mike? Ed? Is anyone here?"

Ed, who'd been sitting at Mike's desk, jumped to
his feet as though there'd been an explosion in the
chair beneath him. Whatever he was holding in his
hand, he tucked under a sheath of papers on Mike's
desk.

"Lexi, what are you doing here? I didn't hear you.

I'm sorry. I should have come out," Ed stammered. Lexi noticed a bead of sweat on his brow.

"I came by to drop off Nancy's sweater."

"I was just taking my break," Ed choked out.

Lexi felt as though she'd caught him doing something wrong, but Ed had every right to be in this office. She took the sweater off her shoulders. "Could you give this to Mike and ask him to return it to Nancy?"

"Sure, sure. No problem." Ed tucked whatever he'd been holding even deeper beneath the papers before taking the sweater from Lexi's hand.

At that moment, a customer drove into the garage and honked the horn. The sound reverberated throughout the building.

"There's my four o'clock appointment," Ed said. "Excuse me for a minute. I'll be right back."

Ed disappeared through the door into the main garage. Lexi frowned. Ed was usually so laid-back and easygoing that his odd behavior seemed very mysterious to her. What was he looking at that made him so jumpy?

Impulsively, without stopping to consider that she might be intruding on Ed's privacy, Lexi lifted the sheath of papers stacked on Mike's desk. There was nothing there but an old book her brother Ben had once given to Todd.

It was a child's book with big pictures and a few words. Lexi remembered reading it to Ben and pointing to the pictures when he was tiny. Ben particularly loved to look at the pictures of the airplane, the barn, the cow, and the rabbit.

That was what Ed was looking at?

What was the big secret about a child's forgotten

book? Lexi was thoroughly puzzled. Why would Ed be looking at that old thing? Even more strange, why would he act so jumpy when caught?

Lexi reached to pick up the book, thought better of it and drew her hand away. She returned the sheath of papers and hid the book once again.

Though Lexi was tempted to ask Ed why he was looking at a child's picture book, she remembered how startled and upset he'd seemed when she'd entered the room.

Lexi backed out of the room and closed the door behind her. "Bye, Ed. Thanks for taking the sweater," she called as she moved toward the exit.

"Bye, Lexi." He waved from beneath the hood of the car. "See you tomorrow."

Lexi was glad to escape into the sunlight without being questioned.

Chapter Ten

Though Lexi was still outside the McNaughtons' back door, she could already hear the noise and chaos inside. Music with a rhythmic beat was playing somewhere upstairs. The TV was reeling out a sit-com, water was running, and Binky was singing loudly and slightly off-key in the kitchen. Lexi drew a deep breath, pressed the doorbell, and waited.

"There you are." Binky threw open the door. She wore a tape measure around her neck and the entire front of her shirt was shot with straight pins.

"You look like a porcupine," Lexi commented.

Binky looked down ruefully at her shirt. "I got into trouble last night. My dad found a straight pin in one of his sandwiches. He told me if I was ever going to sew again, I had to keep track of *every one* of the straight pins I used. I figured the best way to keep track of them would be to keep them on my shirt. Do you think it's a good idea?"

"As long as it doesn't go through the laundry that way."

Binky grabbed Lexi by the hand. "Come into the dining room. I want to show you the dress."

Every counter in the kitchen was strewn with clutter, remnants of beef jerky and peanut brittle.

One area held round dark objects that resembled hockey pucks. Lexi guessed that those were Binky's buns. There were pieces of fabric in a jungle print all over the floor.

In the dining room, however, pieces of Binky's dress were laid out neatly on the table. The pattern was taped to the front of the china cabinet.

"There it is. What do you think?"

Lexi glanced at the pattern and then at the pieces on the table. "Actually, you did a pretty good job, considering. . . ."

"Good job? Do you really think so, Lexi?"

"Sure. As long as you have the pattern pieces straight with the grain of the fabric. . . ."

They began to work, but a commotion in the kitchen distracted Lexi.

"Oh, don't pay any attention." Binky waved a hand in the air. "That's just Egg. He had to run uptown for more groceries. He got hungry while he was making peanut brittle and ate all the peanuts. Ignore the noise."

A scream pierced the air.

Lexi and Binky burst through the dining room door and into the kitchen.

The microwave door was open, and a large puddle of peanut brittle lay cooling on the counter. Egg was submerged head-first in the freezer.

"Ice! Ice! I need ice. I burned myself again. It's bad this time. Help! Ice. Ice."

Lamb chops and a package of frozen peas came flying out of the deep freeze, followed by a package of egg rolls and a pound of hamburger.

"Binky, where are the ice cubes?" Egg had a panicked look on his face. He held his finger in the air.

"I burned myself pouring the peanut brittle out of the pan," he said. "It's burning up."

"Quick, Egg, stick your finger under here." Lexi turned on the cold water faucet. "Binky, you find the ice. I'll get a pan."

Quickly Binky replaced the lamb chops and the peas and pulled out an ice tray. She popped several ice cubes into the mixing bowl Lexi held out for her. Lexi filled the bowl with water, grabbed Egg's wrist, and dunked his entire hand into the bowl. "There. Better?"

"No, it still hurts like crazy."

"Well, you've got to keep your finger cold until it stops burning," Lexi said. "The longer you dance around in the kitchen without cooling that finger off, the longer it's going to hurt."

"If somebody hadn't hidden the ice cubes. . . ." Egg shot his sister an accusing glance.

"Don't look at me. I haven't touched the ice cubes. I haven't been the one cooking today. This mess is all yours." Binky surveyed the devastation in the kitchen.

"I don't know how Mom does it," Egg muttered. "She cooks great meals and she never gets hurt."

"I don't think that cooking is supposed to be a dangerous activity," Lexi commented. "How's the finger?"

Egg pulled it out of the water. "It still hurts."

"Then keep soaking it." Lexi looked around the kitchen. "I'm not sure this is what the people who created this homemaking contest had in mind. After all, this is a home*making* contest, not a home-*breaking* one."

"Will you stick that bowl in the microwave for

me, Lexi?" Egg asked. He inclined his head toward the glass mixing bowl on the counter. "Look on the recipe card to see how many minutes it's supposed to cook. If this batch doesn't work out, I'm sunk."

Lexi noticed puddles of failed peanut brittle resting in foil all over the kitchen. "I thought your father told you not to make any more peanut brittle."

"He said it was all right as long as we hid it before he came home."

Lexi punched in the numbers on the microwave, and the mixture began to cook.

"And when the syrup is done, add the butter and vanilla I have measured out."

"Sounds like you know how to do it," Lexi commented.

"I do. It's just that things keep going wrong."

When the microwave beeped, Egg pulled his hand out of the ice water and wiped it on the leg of his pants. "Let me do it. If it doesn't work this time, I'm giving up." Cautiously, Egg put an oven mitt on each hand and lifted the brittle out of the microwave. He added baking soda and stirred the mixture rapidly until it was foamy. After making sure he'd followed all the instructions on the recipe card, Egg poured the hot goo onto the foil Lexi had spread on the counter.

"How's this?"

"It looks perfect to me, Egg."

"It does, doesn't it?" A grin broke across Egg's face. "That means I did it, Lexi. I made peanut brittle!"

"Egg, you made tons of peanut brittle."

"I made *edible* peanut brittle!"

Binky grabbed Lexi by the hand and pulled her

toward the dining room. "Come on, Lexi, help me do the dress before anything else has a chance to go wrong. Egg's got his peanut brittle. Now we just have to get my project done."

Binky drew Lexi into the dining room and pushed her into a chair in front of the sewing machine. "Now," Binky commanded, "tell me what to do."

By the time Lexi left three hours later, Binky and Egg were both completing their projects. The beef jerky that could pull teeth, hockey puck buns, one final batch of nearly perfect peanut brittle, and half a dress made Egg and Binky beam proudly. Even though most of their projects were twisted, charred, or downright unidentifiable, the pair seemed delighted.

Lexi held her laughter until she reached the street.

Todd pulled into the Leighton driveway just as Lexi arrived at home.

"I've just come from Mike's garage."

"I was there earlier, but I didn't see Mike. Ed was in the office." Lexi looked closely at Todd's somber features. "Is something wrong?"

"I had to get out of there. It was turning into a nuthouse," Todd said bluntly. "I stopped by to see how things were going. Ed was talking to a customer, and Mike was in the office. Everything was going fine until my brother walked out of the office with a stack of car manuals under his arm. Mike handed Ed the books and told him that he might like to read up on the latest stuff. Mike said he was finished with the manuals and told Ed he could keep them as long as he liked. All of a sudden, Ed went ballistic."

"What's the big deal about car manuals?"

"I have no idea, but Ed started acting really weird. He got tense and hostile. He acted as if Mike were going to fire him if he didn't get those manuals read immediately. I know that wasn't Mike's idea at all. Before he met Nancy, Mike spent every night reading about cars and machinery of all sorts. I'm sure my brother was trying to do Ed a favor, but Ed got upset when Mike tried to give him those books.

" 'What are you going to do?' he said, 'Fire me if I don't read them?' "

"Maybe Ed's having a bad day. I know he wasn't himself when I saw him earlier. . . ." Lexi's voice trailed away.

"What do you mean?" Todd's question was sharp. "Did he do something strange?"

Lexi explained how she'd discovered Ed in Mike's office. "I'm not normally a snoop, Todd, but when Ed went into the garage to help the customer, I took a peek at whatever it was he was trying to hide. It was nothing . . . just a child's book, one Ben had left at the garage a long time ago."

"The picture book with airplanes and boats in it?"

"That's the one. If Ed had been trying to read Mike's financial reports, it might have made sense that he'd try to keep it a secret. But looking at one of Ben's old picture books? That makes no sense at all!"

"*Something* is going on. We'll have to figure out what it is. I don't want Ed to quit or Mike to fire him. Ed's the best thing that's happened to this shop in months. Come on, let's go."

When Lexi and Todd arrived, the garage was empty and the office door was closed. Lexi could see through the window that Mike and Ed were having a serious conversation inside.

"Maybe we'd better not interrupt them," Lexi suggested. "They both look upset."

"Do you think they're fighting?"

"Don't look so worried," Lexi consoled Todd. "Your brother Mike thinks Ed is great. He's not going to do anything foolish . . ."

Just then, Ed's voice escalated so that Lexi and Todd could hear him through the door. "Fire me now! Don't wait to see if I get that material read because I'm not going to do it. I'm a good mechanic. I learn on the job. If you can't trust me, get rid of me."

Todd and Lexi looked at each other in dismay. "Come on," Todd said. "I think we'd better talk to these guys."

They burst through the door of Mike's office. Mike was sitting behind the desk, staring at Ed with a baffled expression on his face.

Ed paced in front of the desk, his hands clasped behind his back, his face flushed.

"Ed, I don't see what the big deal is about these car manuals." Mike hardly glanced at Todd and Lexi as they stood in the doorway. "Just because I try to do you a favor to help you keep current, you're blowing your stack. I don't get it. Why are you so bent out of shape over this?"

Ed was agitated, clenching and unclenching his fists and trembling with restrained emotion.

Out of the corner of her eye, Lexi saw the tattered edge of Ben's little picture book peeking out from beneath a pile of papers on the desk. She stared at the corner of the picture book and then at the stacks of complicated car manuals. *It couldn't be*, she thought. *Or could it?*

"Todd!" She grabbed his hand and pulled him into the main garage. "I need to talk to you."

"Can't it wait, Lexi?"

"I don't think so. Something just occurred to me." Quickly she reminded Todd of what she'd seen that afternoon—Ben's picture book and the frantic shame in Ed's eyes when he'd been caught looking at it. "Is it possible, Todd, that Ed's problem is not that he doesn't *want* to read those car manuals, but that he *can't* read them? Maybe Ed can't read."

"It sounds bizarre, but I suppose anything's possible. Come on," Todd said. "We've got to confront him with this."

"Todd, it's just a guess. . . ."

Mike looked up when they re-entered. "Listen you two, I don't have time to talk to you right now. Ed and I are trying to straighten something out. Why don't you come back later?"

"No." Todd shook his head and held his ground. "Lexi has something to say."

"Listen, little brother, it's not very often that I tell you to scram, but I'm telling you now. Get out of here."

"Hey, don't talk to him like that," Ed protested. "We're not getting anywhere with this conversation anyway. They might as well stay."

Mike and Ed glared at each other across the wide expanse of cluttered desk.

Lexi felt her heart in her throat as she began to speak. "Maybe this doesn't have anything to do with what's going on right now," she began. Her voice sounded timid and weak in her ears. "But I just have this hunch. If I'm wrong, I'd like you to tell me so I can forget about it."

Mike gave Lexi and Todd an irritated glare. "I told you that this is not the time."

"Be quiet, Mike," Todd said. Mike raised one eyebrow in surprise.

"Ed, do you remember when I came here this afternoon?" Lexi began unsteadily.

Ed nodded wearily.

"I couldn't find you in the main garage. I walked into Mike's office and you were here, sitting at the desk. You acted very strangely, as if I'd caught you doing something wrong. At first I thought that perhaps you weren't allowed to sit at Mike's desk or that you were reading some financial papers that you weren't supposed to see. That didn't make sense to me, Ed, because you don't seem like a sneaky kind of guy."

Lexi hung her head. "And I'm normally not a sneaky person either, but, after you went into the garage to wait on a customer, I lifted that pile of papers to see what it was you'd been reading. All I could find was one of my little brother Ben's old picture books."

Ed grew pale.

"I thought it was a mistake. Why would you be upset being caught reading a picture book? Why would you even *want* to read a picture book? I've been thinking about it ever since, Ed. No explanation I've come up with has made sense until now."

Lexi glanced at the stack of manuals on the chair beside him. "I think you're upset about Mike asking you to read the manuals, not because you don't *want* to read them, but because you *can't*. Were you trying to teach yourself to read with my little brother's book?"

Ed sank against his chair like a deflating balloon, a shriveled and withered shadow of his usual self. Mike jumped up from his chair and put his hands on his desk.

"That's ridiculous, Lexi. Not only that, it's downright insulting."

Mike stopped talking at the sound of Ed's soft weeping. "Ed. . . ?"

Ed sat hunched over in his chair, grinding the heels of his hands into his eye sockets.

"You mean she's *right*?"

Ed looked up, and the despair on his face was painful to see. "I've kept my secret so long, Lexi. I've always been terrified that I'd be found out, but I never expected it would be you."

"I'm sorry, Ed."

"I've been waiting for this," Ed admitted. "It's affected my every waking hour. Not being able to read has filled my life with shame and insecurity. I've felt like such a failure."

"Ed, you're not a failure. You're the best mechanic I've ever seen," Mike interjected.

"Yeah, right," Ed said with a twist of his lip. "You mean I'm the most *hardworking* mechanic you've ever seen. All my life I've had to make up for what I lacked with extra effort."

"Why didn't you just tell me?"

"And see the look on your face? Hear the words, 'Sorry, I don't think I can use you.' No thanks. I've gone that route before. It's too painful. Knowing that I can't read is bad enough. Having others know it so they can pity or laugh at me is too hard."

He looked down at the toes of his work-worn boots. Lexi could read the shame in his eyes. "It's so embarrassing when I can't read a simple sign that's so obvious to everyone else. When I have to use the rest room, I stand outside the doors waiting to see who comes out, a man or a woman. And when I go to a grocery store, I buy everything by the pictures on the front of the packages. If there's not a picture, I don't buy it because I don't know what I'm getting. I hate grocery stores that have lots of selections. It's too confusing. It used to be easier to buy milk before they started putting orange juice in the same kind of packaging."

Ed's lips twisted in an unhappy grimace. "Imagine the first time I poured orange juice on my corn flakes."

"Oh, Ed." Lexi's heart ached for him.

"Remember when you asked me to fill out an application form for this job?" Ed asked. "I nearly panicked and ran out. I only stayed because I knew if I could take the form home, I could get help from my neighbor. He's been helping me with my business for years. I've told him my eyes are bad, so he doesn't mind reading things aloud and filling in the blanks for me. He's even purchased birthday cards for me. I don't dare pick them out myself. What if I sent a get-well card or an anniversary card instead?" Ed drooped even lower in the chair. "My whole life has been lived on the edge. Every minute I've been afraid of making a mistake, of being found out."

"You should have told me. We could have helped you."

"Told you? And risk being fired from the best job I've ever had? Are you crazy? Why would you want to help me? It's too much trouble. Anyway, I don't think there is help for me anymore."

Mike gave a disgusted snort. "That's how much you know about anything. Our mother belongs to a group of volunteers who teach illiterate persons to read. It's one of her favorite projects. She's done it for years."

"Mom loves it," Todd added. "There are several people in Cedar River who've gone through the program."

"There are?" For the first time, Lexi saw a flicker of hope in Ed's eyes.

"It's not all your fault that you can't read, Ed. Somewhere along the line you must have fallen through the cracks in the educational system. Talk to my mom. She can tell you how to apply for this program. You might have to wait awhile to get started. There are a lot of people on a waiting list."

"You're sure I'm not the only one?"

"The only one who can't read?" Mike shook his head. "Of course not. You mean you actually thought you were?"

"I didn't know." Ed hung his head. "I never dared talk about it to anyone."

Mike walked around the desk and put his arm across Ed's shoulders. "Listen, there are a lot of things that you could do wrong that might cost you your job, but not being able to read isn't one of them. Not here. Not with me. We'll talk to my mother about getting you signed up for the literacy program. We can do it tonight, if you want."

Mike's kindness and generosity were too much for Ed to bear. He broke down and sobbed like a child.

Todd put his arm around Lexi and held her close. There was nothing to say or do except watch all the years of pain being shed with Ed's tears.

When Ed finally composed himself, he gave Mike a lopsided grin. "You have no idea how much this means to me. I've been pretending all my life. When I go to a restaurant, I always order the special. That way, I don't have to look at the menu. I've been pretending so long that I'm exhausted from it."

"You don't have to pretend for us anymore," Mike said frankly. "You can rest now. You're with friends."

Ed stared at Mike for a long moment. "Are you sure? Absolutely sure? Because if you aren't, I'll just pick up my stuff and go. I will understand why you wouldn't want a guy in this shop who doesn't know how to read. I could make a big mistake. I could cost you money."

"Ed, you work with your hands. You're a top-notch mechanic. If you can't figure something out, come to me. I'll read the manual to you. I'll help you. Besides, you've underestimated my mother. If we put her and her friends on your case, you're going to be reading before you know what hit you."

"And I can help you, Ed." Lexi looked shyly at Todd. "We both could. Maybe you'll have to do flash cards or something. The nights that you're not working with a tutor, we could help you study."

"You'd do that for me?"

"Sure. It would be great," Todd responded. "We waste a lot of time at the Hamburger Shack after school. We might as well be here helping you."

Ed's shoulders shook, his chest heaved, and again tears streamed down his cheeks in a flood.

Mike, Todd, and Lexi watched helplessly as tears of relief racked his body. When he looked up, there was an expression on his face that reminded Lexi of the sun beaming through fast-evaporating clouds.

"Thank you. Thanks to all of you." Ed grabbed Mike's hand and began to pump it hard and fast. Then he threw his arms around Todd and slapped him across the back until Todd nearly choked. Finally Ed drew Lexi to him and held her hands in his own.

"You don't know how much this means to me. You can't. All my life I've thought I was worthless and stupid. A second-class citizen. And today you've made me feel like I'm real. Like I have hope."

Lexi put her arms around Ed and gave him a hug.

Ed beamed broadly. "You know that old saying, 'Today is the first day of the rest of your life'? Well, thanks to you guys, I feel like today *is* the first day of my life. You've given me a fresh start. Thank you . . . thank you."

Chapter Eleven

"Why is the gymnasium locked?" Todd wondered as he gathered his books for his next class. "I usually take a shortcut through there, but all the doors were closed."

"Tonight is the homemaking contest," Lexi said. "Have you already forgotten about Egg and Binky's big domestic adventure? The doors open at six. That's when we get to see all the entries."

"Big time. Sounds like fun to me." Jennifer joined them. "Are you guys coming back to the school tonight?"

"I don't want to miss this," Todd said. "Besides, I think my friend Egg will need a little moral support."

"Let's meet outside the front door to the school at six," Jennifer suggested.

"It's a plan. See you then."

———

Promptly at six, Jennifer, Lexi, and Todd arrived at the school.

"Are we ready for this?" Todd wondered aloud.

Lexi chewed worriedly on her bottom lip. "I hope Egg and Binky don't make absolute fools of themselves. They've worked so hard. They deserve some sort of recognition."

"If they've cooked anything edible, they might have a chance," Jennifer said. "It's just a little doubtful whether either Egg or Binky could produce something that another human being could eat and still live."

"Well, here goes." Todd grabbed both girls by the hand and pulled them into the school. The gymnasium was set with long tables covered with white paper tablecloths. Lexi groaned as she looked at the rows and rows of beautiful baked products on display.

"Where's Egg?" Todd asked, uninterested in anything but his friend.

"He's set up at the far end of these tables," Jennifer said. "He's waving at us. Come on."

"Hi, guys. I'm glad you came." Egg's teddy bear was sitting on a table with a tag indicating which category of the contest he'd entered. Under name of item submitted, Egg had written "stuffed baboon."

"I see your teddy bear had a species change," Todd commented.

"We had a hunch the judges would know what a stuffed teddy bear looked like, but we thought maybe we could trick them into thinking this was a baboon. Not bad, huh?"

"And this is your peanut brittle?" Jennifer poked at the caramel-colored candy. "Looks good."

"You can have some after the contest."

Lexi leaned over and looked closely at the peanut brittle. She was positive she saw a tooth mark or two marring the candy, but wisely, she kept her opinion to herself.

"Egg! Your beef jerky! There's a ribbon beside it."

Egg beamed proudly. "I know. Isn't it great? I won!"

"You won a prize? You're kidding." Todd stared at the little pile of dark rubble. "But why?"

"I was the only one who entered the category," Egg explained. "But I don't care how I got a ribbon. Just the fact that I got it is good enough for me."

Todd slapped Egg on the back. "Maybe you're on your way to the water park after all."

Egg held up two fingers crossed at the center. "I'm keeping these crossed just in case."

"Where's Binky?" Lexi asked.

"Over there."

When Binky saw them, she came dashing across the floor. "Guess what? My dress got an honorable mention in the sewing category! Isn't that wonderful?" She flung her arms around Lexi. "And it's all thanks to you. If you hadn't told me what to do, I never would have finished that stupid dress."

"So you each got a ribbon. Impressive."

"I'm not sure we can win any big prizes, but I hope we win something."

That moment, one of the contest judges came to the microphone to announce the prize winners. It was a sad moment for Binky and Egg when they saw the water park tickets and the boom box go to someone else.

"All this work," Binky moaned, "and we didn't make it."

"They aren't done giving prizes yet, Binky. Don't be discouraged. Maybe you'll get something."

As the list of names and prizes continued, Binky and Egg began to look more and more dejected.

"They're not going to call our names," Binky said morosely. "I just know it."

"And now, for the final prizes. In the camping competition, first prize has gone to Mr. Edward Mc-Naughton for his delicious submission of beef jerky."

"Hey, that's me!" Egg perked up immediately.

"And Mr. McNaughton, I am happy to say that you have won this very fine gift from one of our local hardware stores." The judge held out a large, gaily-wrapped package. Egg immediately trotted to the front to claim his prize.

"And, to the runner-up in the sewing category, Miss Bonita McNaughton, we would like to present you with a pair of sewing shears. I hope you will be able to use these in all your future sewing projects."

"You mean you're going to sew again, Binky?" Jennifer hissed. Binky gave her a dirty look. She graciously tried to hide her disappointment, but as soon as she returned from the podium, her gaze fell on Egg's large gift box.

"Open it, Egg. That's a huge box. I bet there's something really neat inside."

Without any more encouragement, Egg tore into the gift box, expecting something marvelous inside. Camping equipment, perhaps. Or at least a new electronic gadget.

The expression on his face was heartbreaking as he lifted a set of mixing bowls and a recipe book out of the box.

"Mixing bowls? A recipe book? Sewing shears? Now you guys can really get domestic," Jennifer said with a giggle.

"All this trouble, Binky, and what do we get? This stuff. No trip to a water park. No boom box. Stuff to cook and sew with! What a stupid idea you had," Egg growled. "Whatever made you think that we should enter this contest?"

"Leave her alone, Egg," Todd said. "She's disappointed enough already without you helping her." Todd turned to Binky. "Well, Bink, did you learn anything from all of this?"

"Actually, I did."

"You did?" Egg was surprised. "I never thought you learned from anything you did."

"First of all, I learned that I really do like to cook. It's fun." She eyed Egg's recipe book and mixing bowls. "I wouldn't be complaining if I'd won those. I think that's a neat gift."

"You can have them," Egg said.

"And the other thing I learned," Binky continued, "is that my brother messes up everything he does. He can't get anything straight. Whoever thought of using a baboon as a child's toy? I mean, really."

"It was your idea."

"Only because it didn't look enough like a teddy bear to pass for one."

"Don't make fun of my baboon."

"Don't you tell me what to do or I'm going to hit you over the head with one of my buns."

"Hockey pucks, you mean."

"Whatever. It's going to hurt."

"Here they go again," Todd and Lexi groaned together.

"Let's get out of here," Todd said.

"Those two are hopeless."

"You go ahead," Jennifer said, "I'll stay and break up the fight. I'd like to see how this one turns out."

Todd and Lexi left the gym laughing. Behind

them they could hear Egg and Binky pointing out the various flaws in each other's projects.

"That argument could take a long time," Todd commented. "There are a lot of things wrong with those projects they turned in." He glanced at his watch. "It's early yet. Do you want to stop and see Mike and Nancy?"

"Why not? I don't have much homework tonight," Lexi agreed.

When they arrived at Nancy's house, Ed's car was in the driveway. It was Mike who answered the front door. "Hi, come on in. We're all in the kitchen."

"It smells great in here," Todd exclaimed as they walked into the warm and friendly room.

Ed was standing at the counter, an apron around his waist and a wide grin on his face.

"What are you doing?"

"I'm learning how to read a recipe for chocolate chip cookies," he said proudly. "I've always wanted to make them at home, but I've never dared ask anyone to help me." Ed held up a recipe card. "See? Nancy's drawn little pictures on the card next to the directions."

"We've read through the card several times so Ed practically has it memorized. Now he can practice reading and do some baking at the same time."

Nancy, who was seated at a stool at the end of the counter, looked up and smiled sweetly. "He's not going to need those cards long. Ed is so smart. I wish he'd told us about his problem the day we met. We've wasted a lot of time. He could have been reading my biology books by now."

Ed pulled a pan of freshly baked cookies out of the oven and carefully moved them to a waiting rack to cool. "How did your friends do in their contest?"

Todd and Lexi told them about Egg's mixing bowls and Binky's sewing shears.

They had been laughing and talking for several minutes before Lexi realized that Nancy hadn't said anything for quite a while. She was unusually quiet tonight, and she looked very pale. Was Nancy ill? None of the guys had noticed, so it surely couldn't be anything serious. Still, Nancy seemed paler than usual and perhaps a little thinner. It was difficult for Lexi to throw herself wholeheartedly back into the conversation. For a while everything had seemed so perfect. Now a single question kept rolling around in her mind. What was wrong with Nancy?

What is wrong with Nancy? Find out in Cedar River Daydreams 20, *The Discovery*.

Egg McNaughton's Peanut Brittle Recipe

1½ cups peanuts (skinned and raw preferred, but salted will work)
1 cup granulated sugar
½ cup light corn syrup
pinch of salt
1 tablespoon butter
1 teaspoon vanilla extract
1 teaspoon baking soda

Mix peanuts, sugar, corn syrup, and salt in a glass mixing bowl. Microwave 7–9 minutes on high (mixture should be bubbling and peanuts brown). Quickly stir in butter and vanilla. Cook 2–3 minutes longer. Add baking soda and stir quickly, just until mixture is foamy. Pour immediately onto greased baking sheet (or aluminum foil). Let cool for 15 minutes or longer. Break into pieces.

Enjoy!